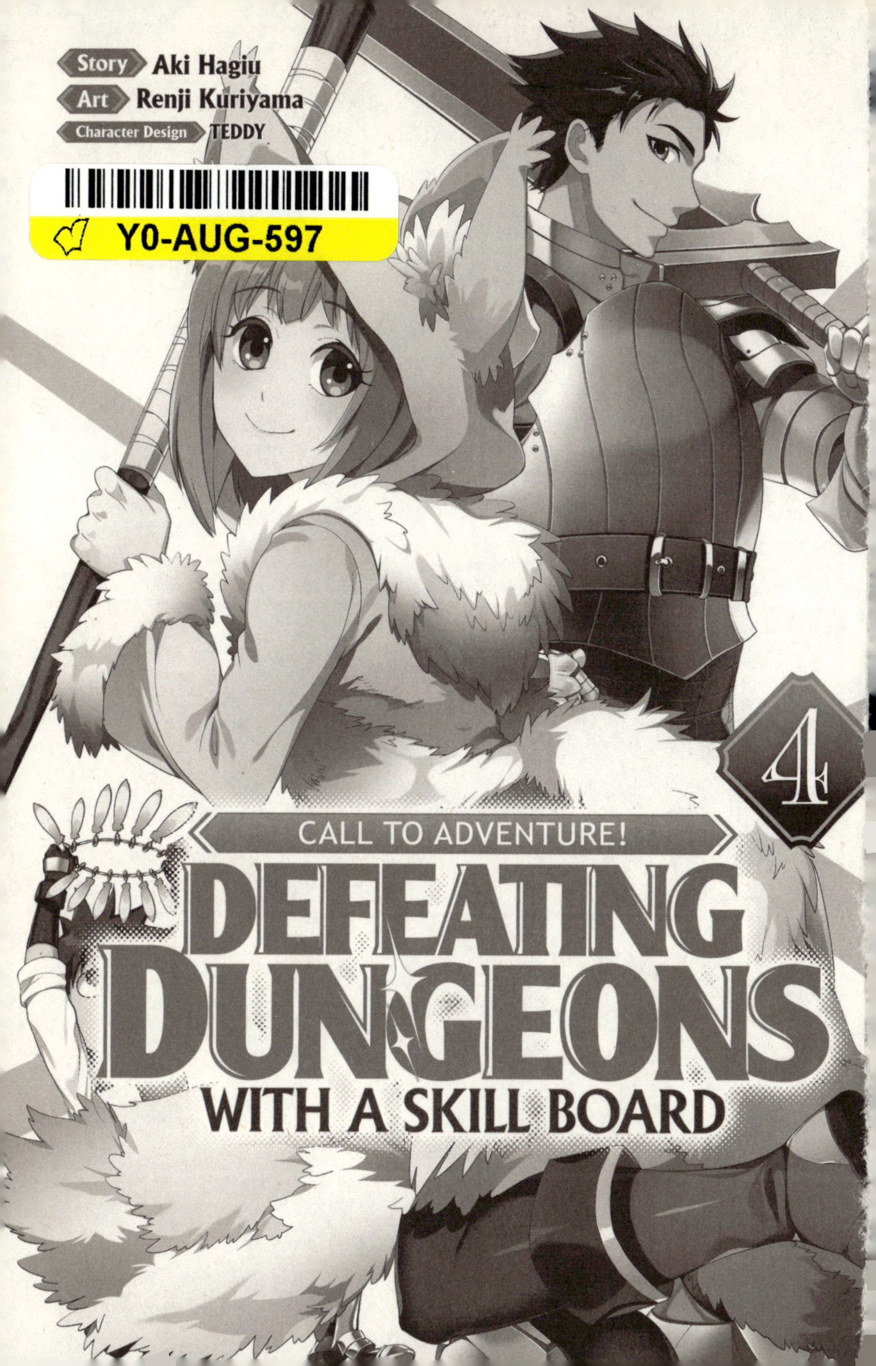
Story Aki Hagiu
Art Renji Kuriyama
Character Design TEDDY
4
CALL TO ADVENTURE!
DEFEATING DUNGEONS
WITH A SKILL BOARD

CONTENTS

Chapter 16	003
Chapter 17	037
Chapter 18	068
Chapter 19	099
Chapter 20	131

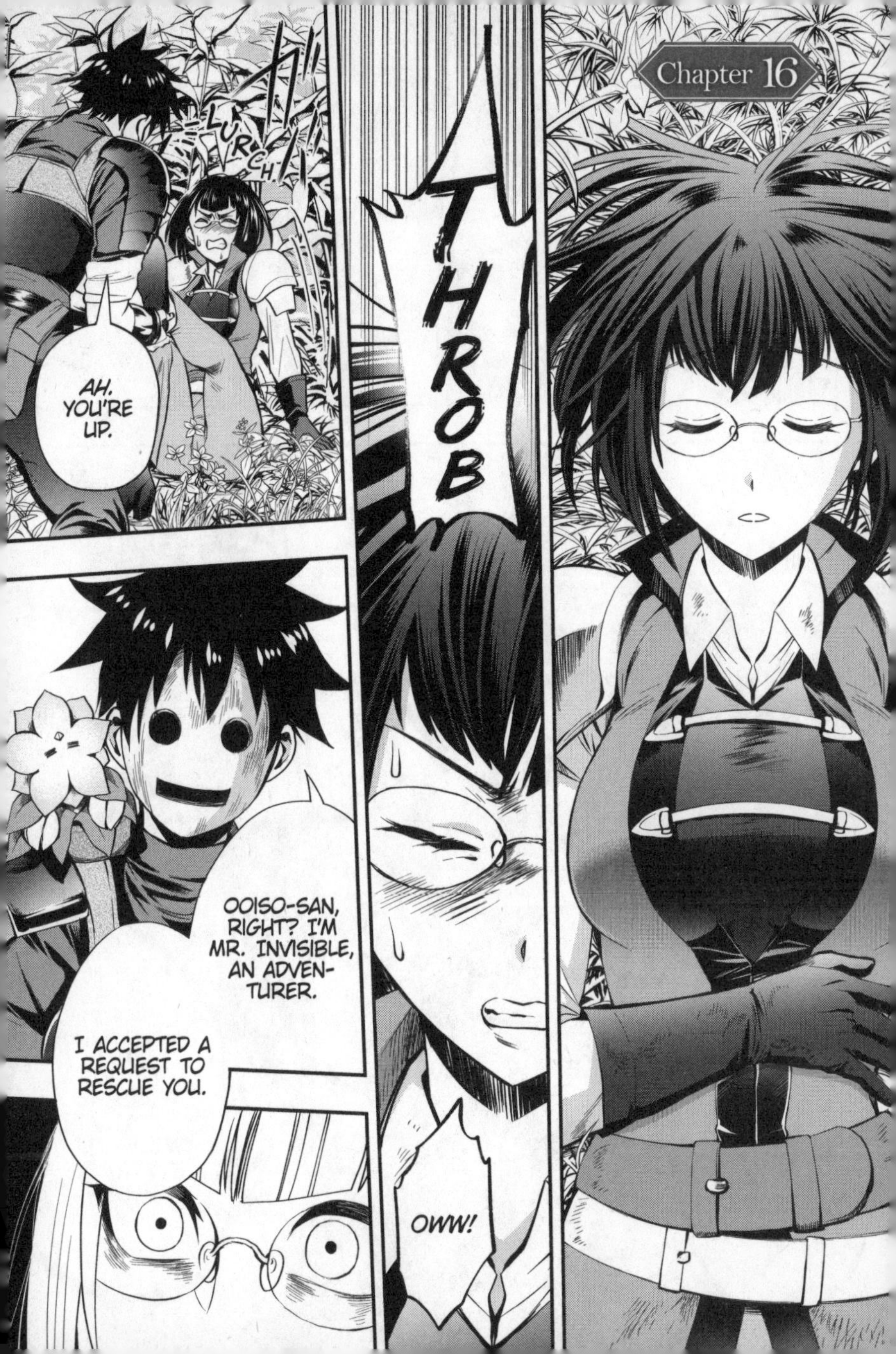
Chapter 16
THROB
OWW!
LURCH
AH. YOU'RE UP.
OOISO-SAN, RIGHT? I'M MR. INVISIBLE, AN ADVENTURER.
I ACCEPTED A REQUEST TO RESCUE YOU.

WOBBLE
WHOA!
DON'T PASS OUT! CARRYING YOU'D BE TOO MUCH WORK.
SHAKE
SHAKE
AH!
GET BACK, MONSTER!!
DUN
I BET YOU'RE PLANNING TO VIOLATE ME IN ALL SORTS OF WAYS.
NGH! JUST KILL ME INSTEAD!!
SORRY TO INTERRUPT YOUR DELUSIONS, BUT CAN YOU STAND?

HUH?
THIS IS KAREN.
LIKE I SAID, WE ACCEPTED A REQUEST TO SAVE YOU.
A RE-QUEST?
YES.
THE EMPLOYEES OF ICHIBISHI AWAIT YOUR SAFE RETURN.
BUT MY LEG IS...
H-HUH?
IT DOESN'T HURT!
I USED A HEALING TONIC ON IT! HOW DO YOU FEEL?

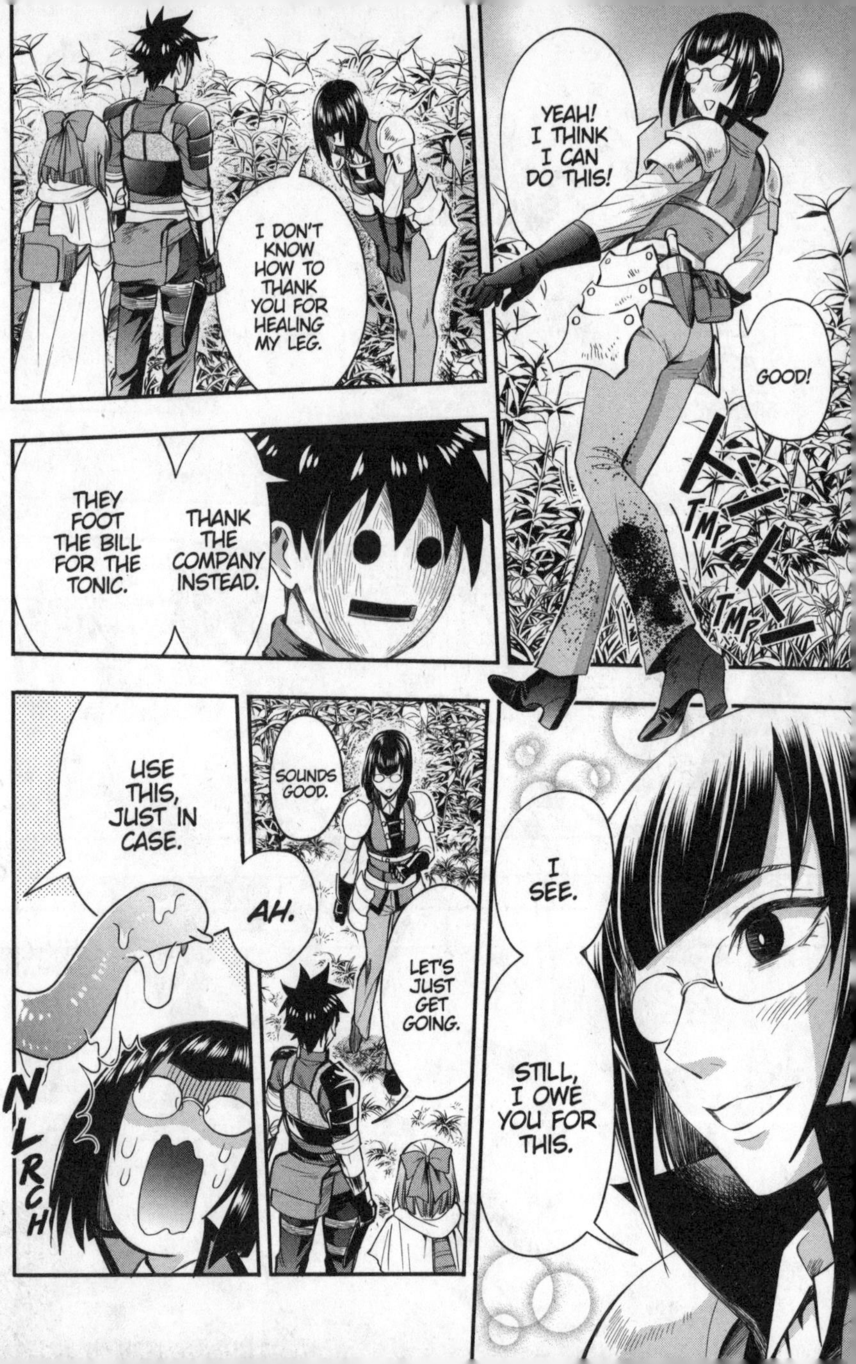
YEAH! I THINK I CAN DO THIS!
GOOD!
TMP TMP TMP
I DON'T KNOW HOW TO THANK YOU FOR HEALING MY LEG.
THANK THE COMPANY INSTEAD.
THEY FOOT THE BILL FOR THE TONIC.
I SEE.
STILL, I OWE YOU FOR THIS.
LET'S JUST GET GOING.
SOUNDS GOOD.
USE THIS, JUST IN CASE.
AH.
NLRCH

THERE'S THE GATE.

Gates

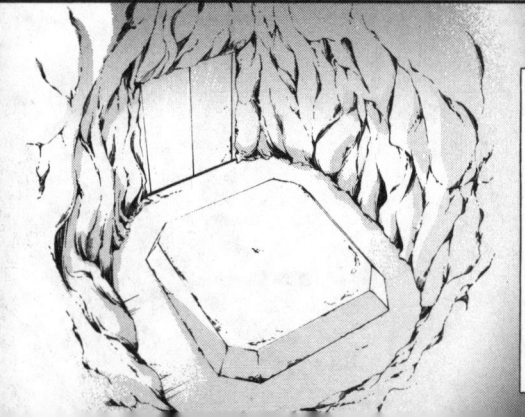

Devices that allow movement between the dungeon's levels. They only operate on levels an Adventurer has personally visited.

<From the Call wiki>

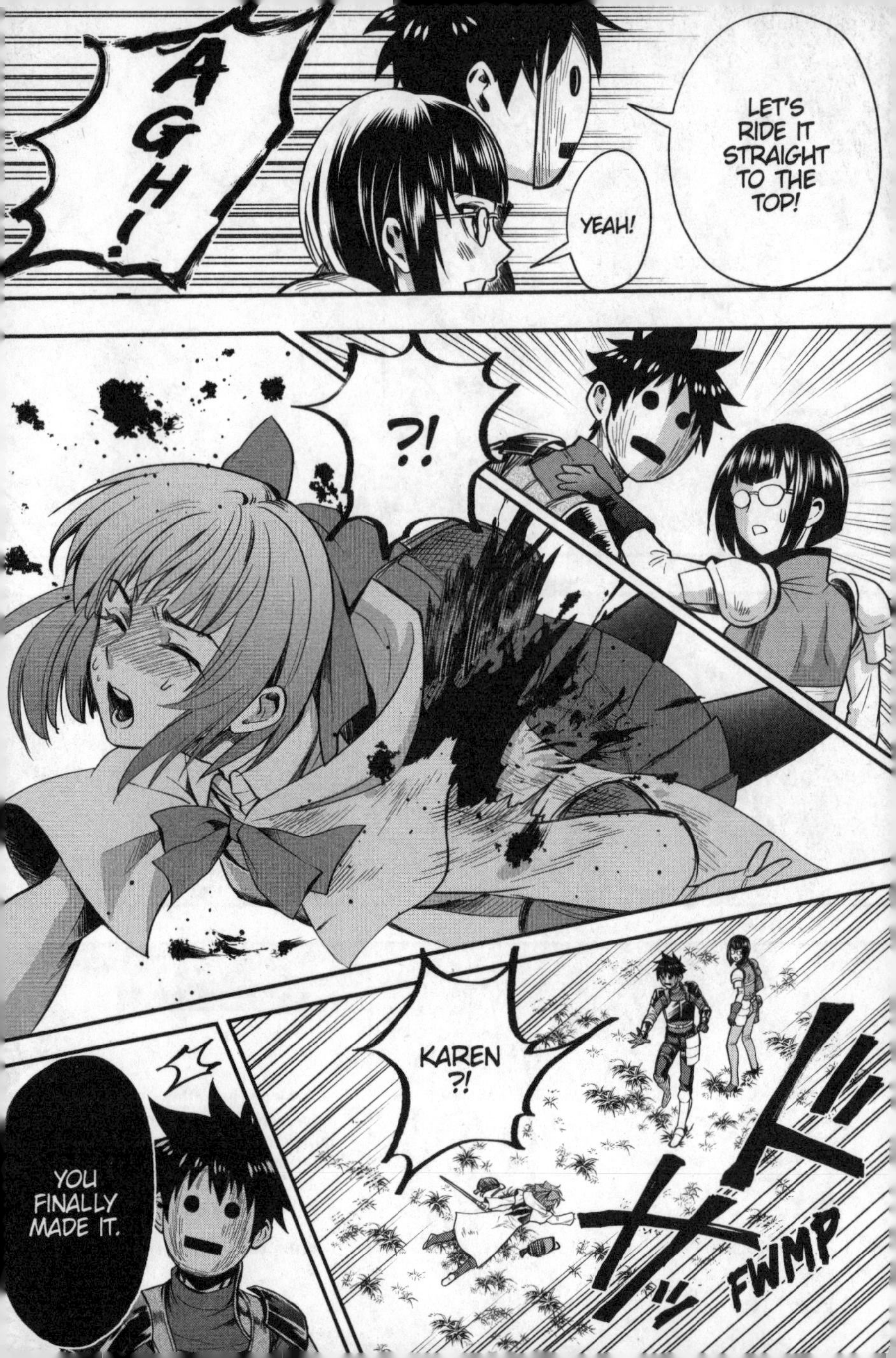
LET'S RIDE IT STRAIGHT TO THE TOP!
YEAH!
AGH!
?!
KAREN ?!
FWMP
YOU FINALLY MADE IT.

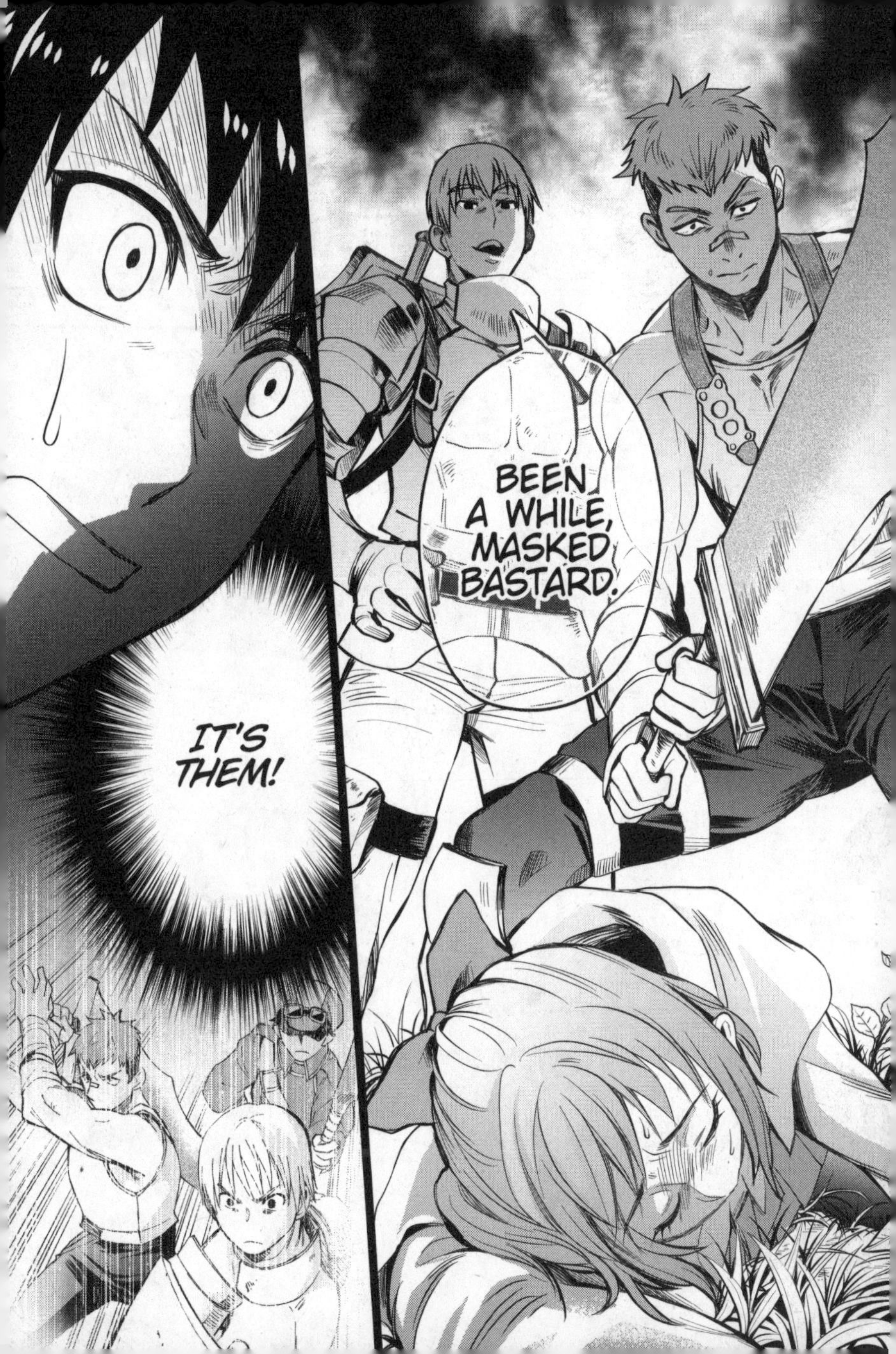
BEEN A WHILE, MASKED BASTARD.
IT'S THEM!

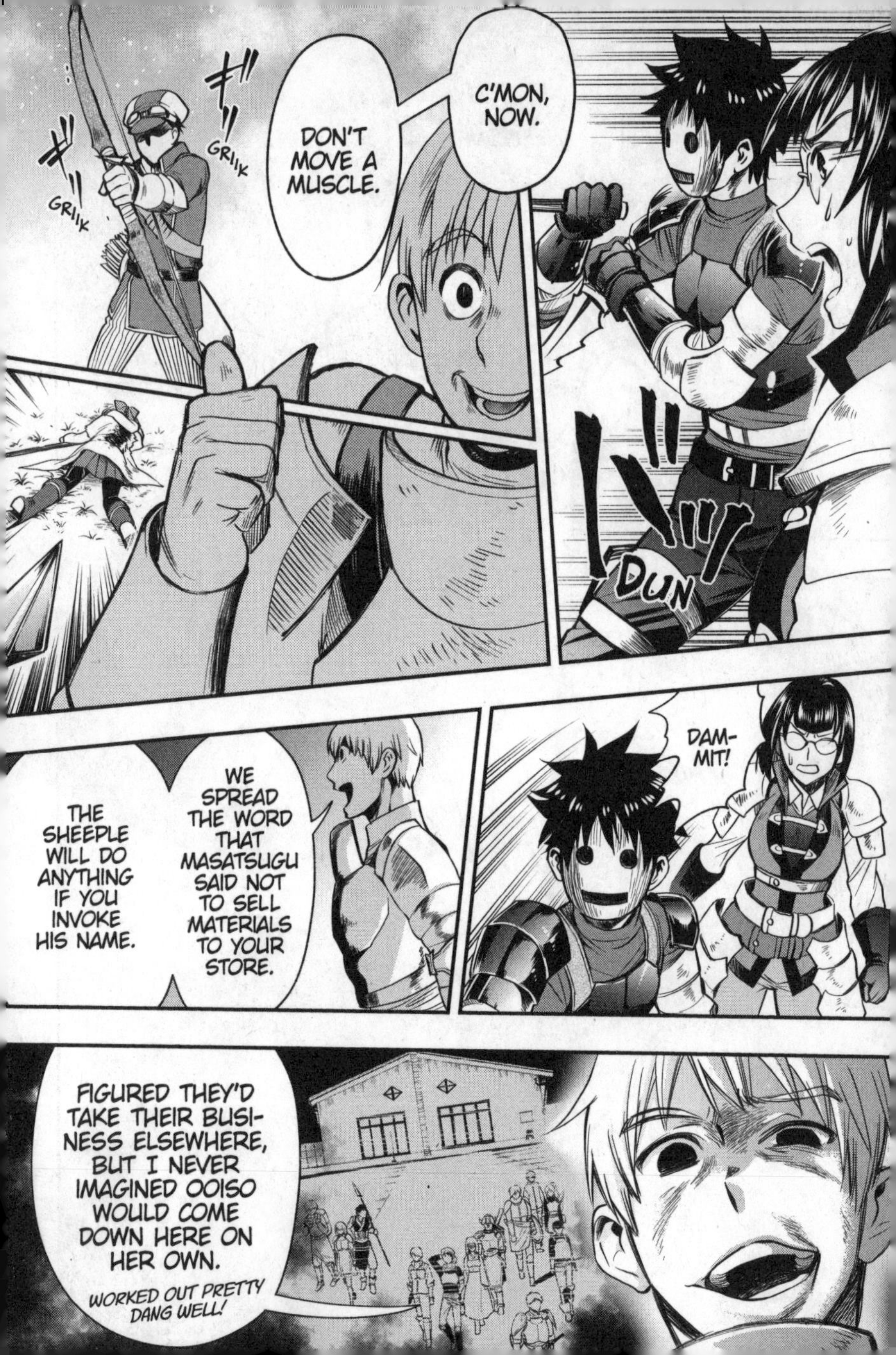
DUN
C'MON, NOW.
DON'T MOVE A MUSCLE.
GRIIK
GRIIK
DAM-MIT!
WE SPREAD THE WORD THAT MASATSUGU SAID NOT TO SELL MATERIALS TO YOUR STORE.
THE SHEEPLE WILL DO ANYTHING IF YOU INVOKE HIS NAME.
FIGURED THEY'D TAKE THEIR BUSI-NESS ELSEWHERE, BUT I NEVER IMAGINED OOISO WOULD COME DOWN HERE ON HER OWN.
WORKED OUT PRETTY DANG WELL!

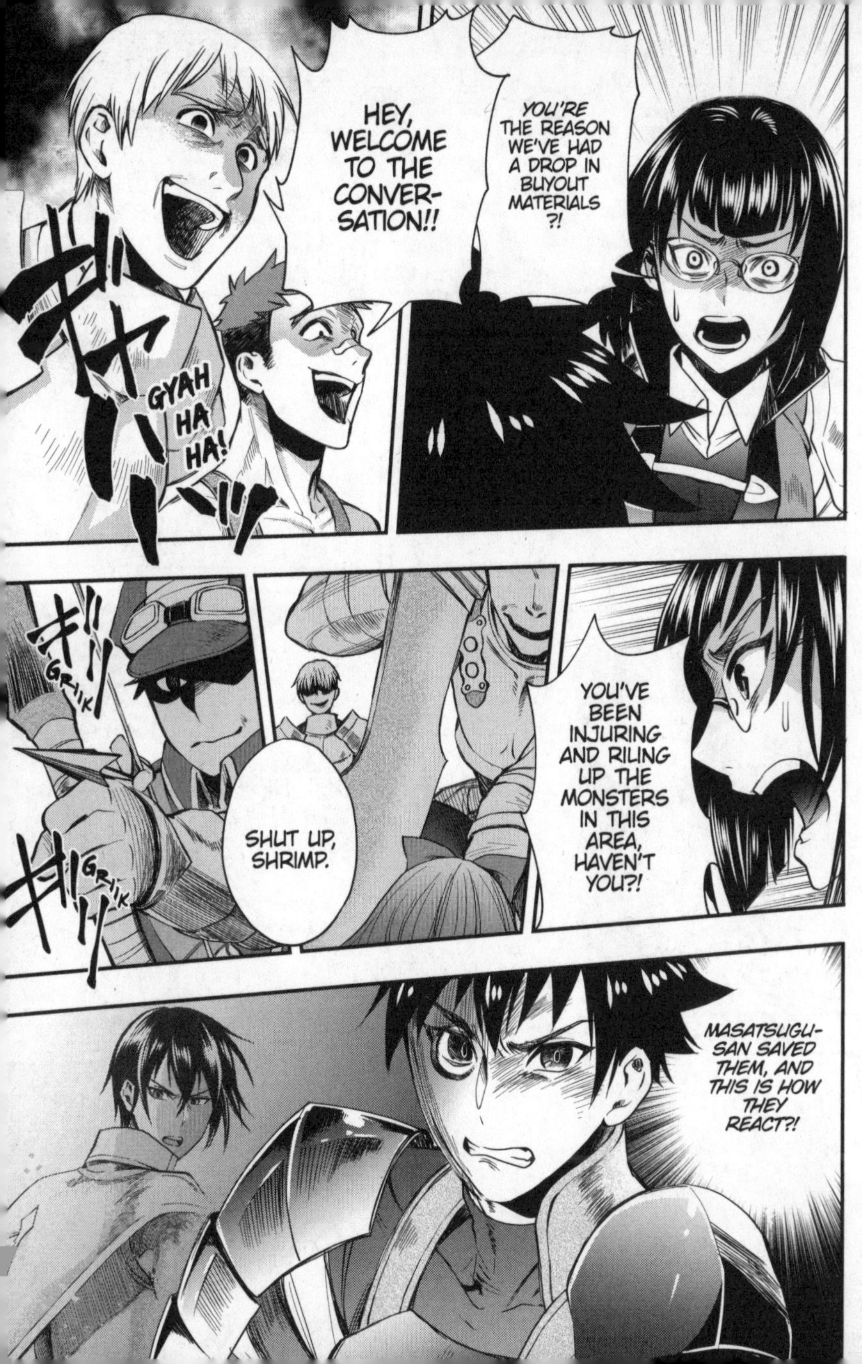
YOU'RE THE REASON WE'VE HAD A DROP IN BUYOUT MATERIALS ?!
HEY, WELCOME TO THE CONVER-SATION!!
GYAH HA HA!
YOU'VE BEEN INJURING AND RILING UP THE MONSTERS IN THIS AREA, HAVEN'T YOU?!
SHUT UP, SHRIMP.
GRIIK
GRIIK
MASATSUGU-SAN SAVED THEM, AND THIS IS HOW THEY REACT?!

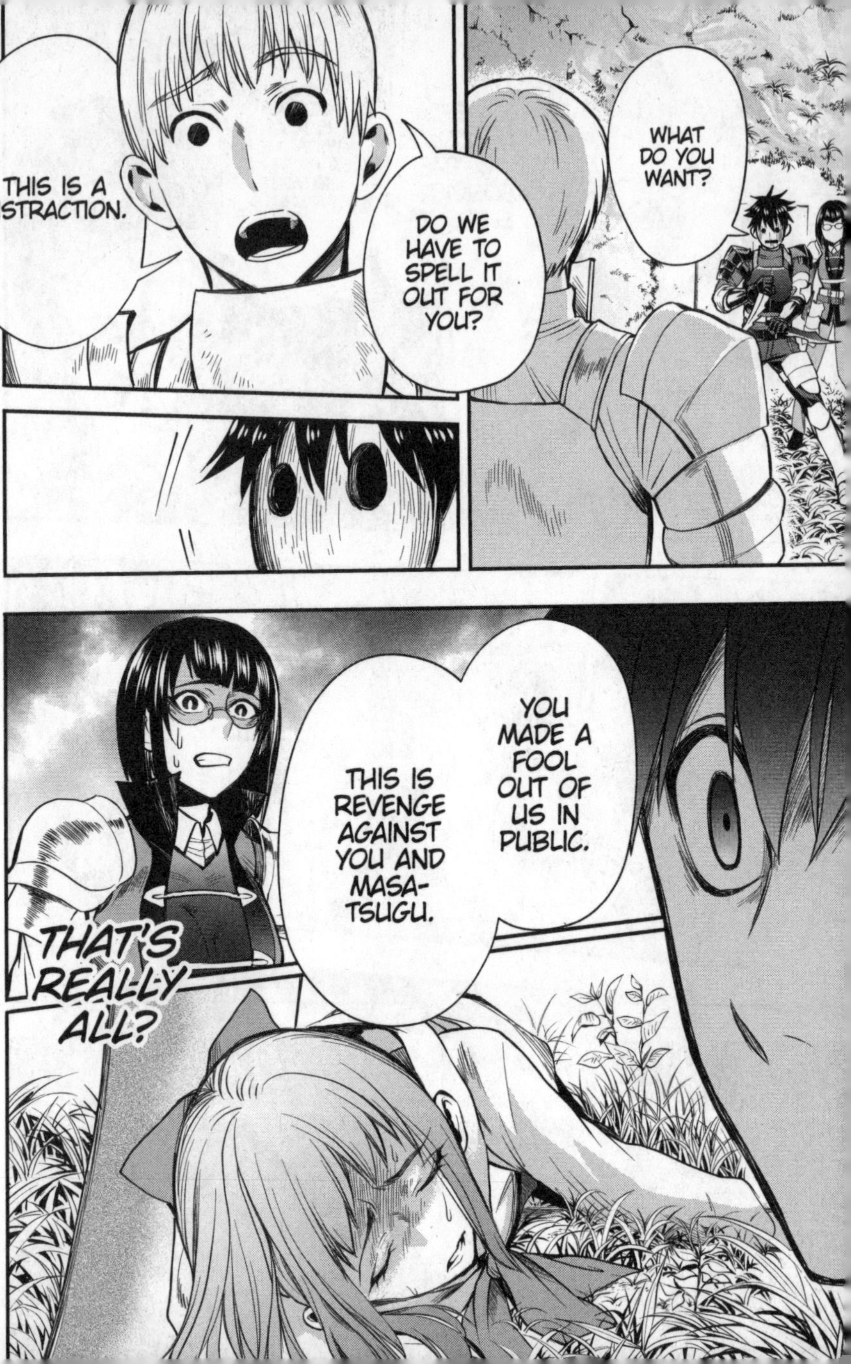
WHAT DO YOU WANT?
DO WE HAVE TO SPELL IT OUT FOR YOU?
THIS IS A DISTRACTION.
YOU MADE A FOOL OUT OF US IN PUBLIC.
THIS IS REVENGE AGAINST YOU AND MASA-TSUGU.
THAT'S REALLY ALL?

THIS IS RIDICULOUS! YOU WON'T GET AWAY WITH THIS!

WHY'RE YOU MAKING US SOUND LIKE CRIMINALS?

WE'RE NOT DOING ANYTHING WRONG.

HOW CAN YOU SAY THAT?!

WHEN I REPORT THIS, YOU'LL BE STRIPPED OF YOUR RIGHTS AS ADVENTURERS AND--!

HUH?

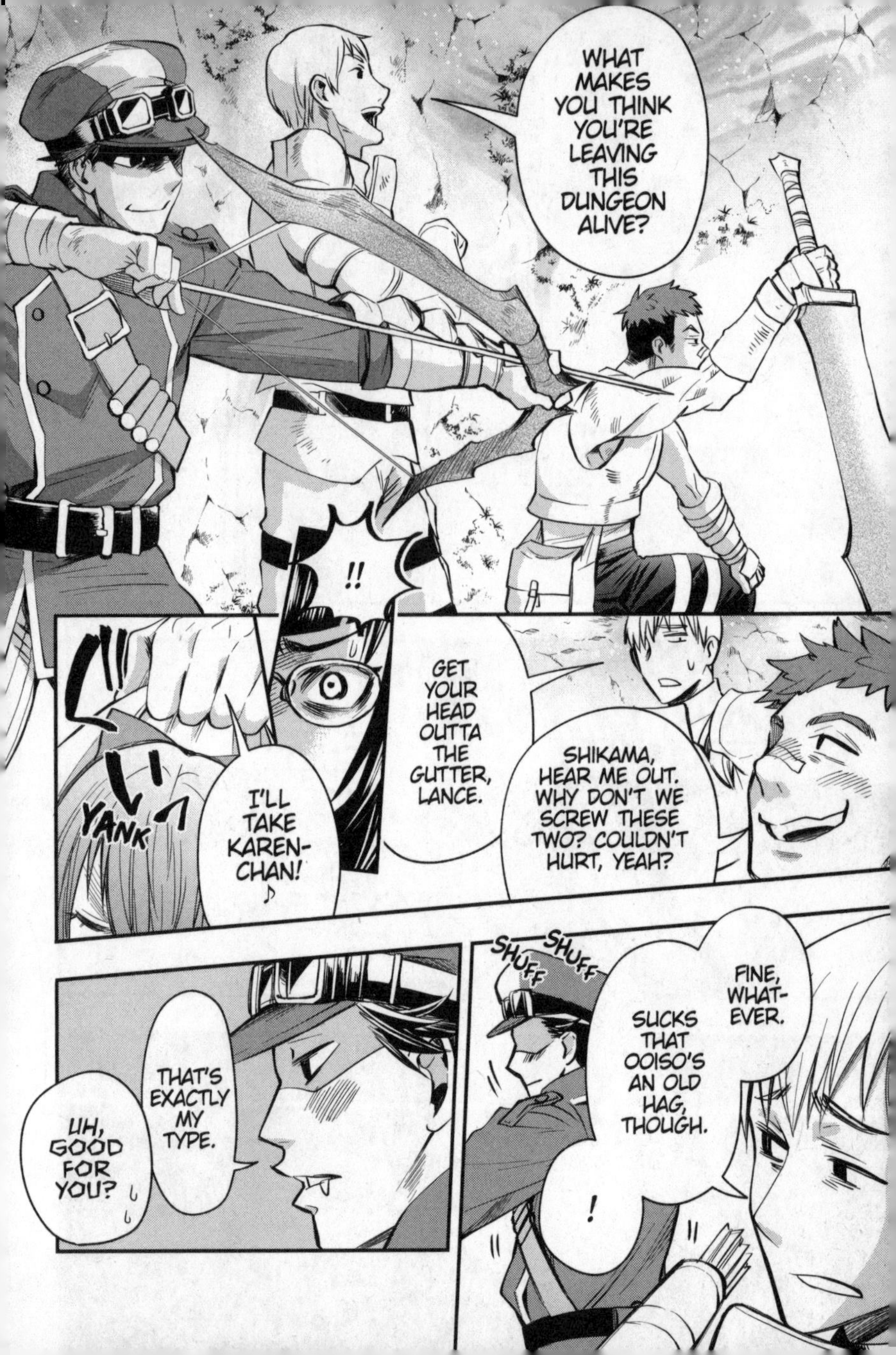
WHAT MAKES YOU THINK YOU'RE LEAVING THIS DUNGEON ALIVE?
SHIKAMA, HEAR ME OUT. WHY DON'T WE SCREW THESE TWO? COULDN'T HURT, YEAH?
GET YOUR HEAD OUTTA THE GUTTER, LANCE.
!!
I'LL TAKE KAREN-CHAN! ♪
YANK
SHUFF SHUFF
FINE, WHATEVER.
SUCKS THAT OOISO'S AN OLD HAG, THOUGH.
!
THAT'S EXACTLY MY TYPE.
UH, GOOD FOR YOU?

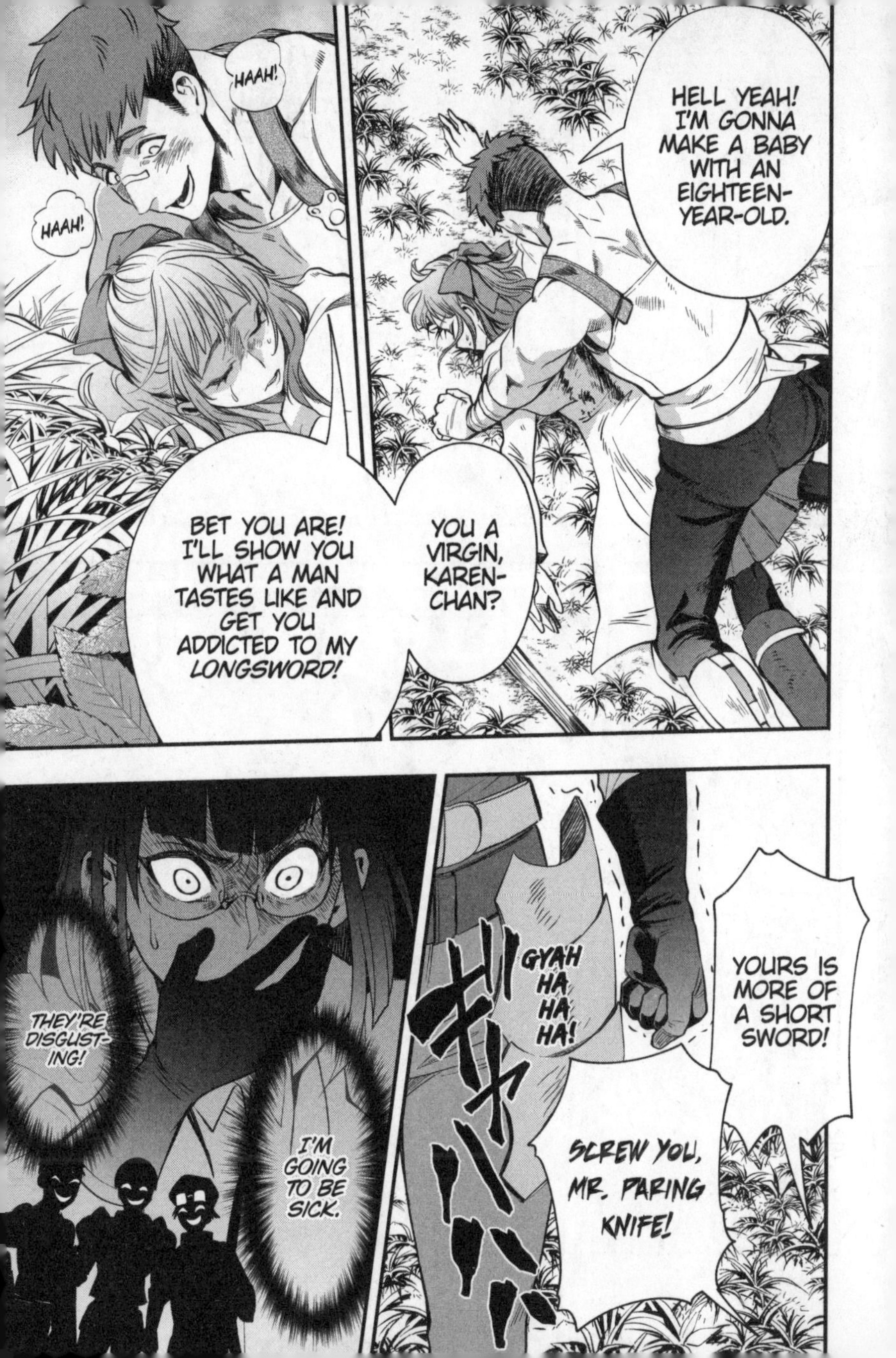
HELL YEAH! I'M GONNA MAKE A BABY WITH AN EIGHTEEN-YEAR-OLD.
HAAH!
HAAH!
YOU A VIRGIN, KAREN-CHAN?
BET YOU ARE! I'LL SHOW YOU WHAT A MAN TASTES LIKE AND GET YOU ADDICTED TO MY *LONGSWORD!*
YOURS IS MORE OF A SHORT SWORD!
SCREW YOU, MR. PARING KNIFE!
GYAH HA HA HA!
THEY'RE DISGUSTING!
I'M GOING TO BE SICK.

HOW ARE SUCH VULGAR PEOPLE ADVEN-TURERS?!
KNGH...
GRN GRN GRN
AS FOR THE MASKED JERK, HOW ABOUT...
FLINCH
NO! DON'T MOVE!
WE CHOP HIS DAMN HEAD OFF?!!!
THWUK
ZA-ZSHH

MR. INVISIBLE, RUN AND CONTACT THE AUTHORI--!
FWP
SILENCE
H-HEY! HE'S GONE!
SINCE WHEN?!!
WE'RE SCREWED IF HE GETS TO THE SURFACE!!
DAMMIT!!!
FEED THE WOMEN TO THE MONSTERS!!
BUT I WANNA HAVE FUN WITH KAREN-CHAN!!

SCREW THAT!
WE NEED TO ERASE THE EVIDENCE BEFORE THE POLICE SHOW UP!
THAT WAY, WE CAN SAY HE'S A LIAR!
FINE.
GUESS I'LL HAVE TO SWING MY LONG-SWORD AROUND THE CLUB TONIGHT.
KNCH
KNCH
MY PRETTY HOLE.
FARE-WELL...
CHAK

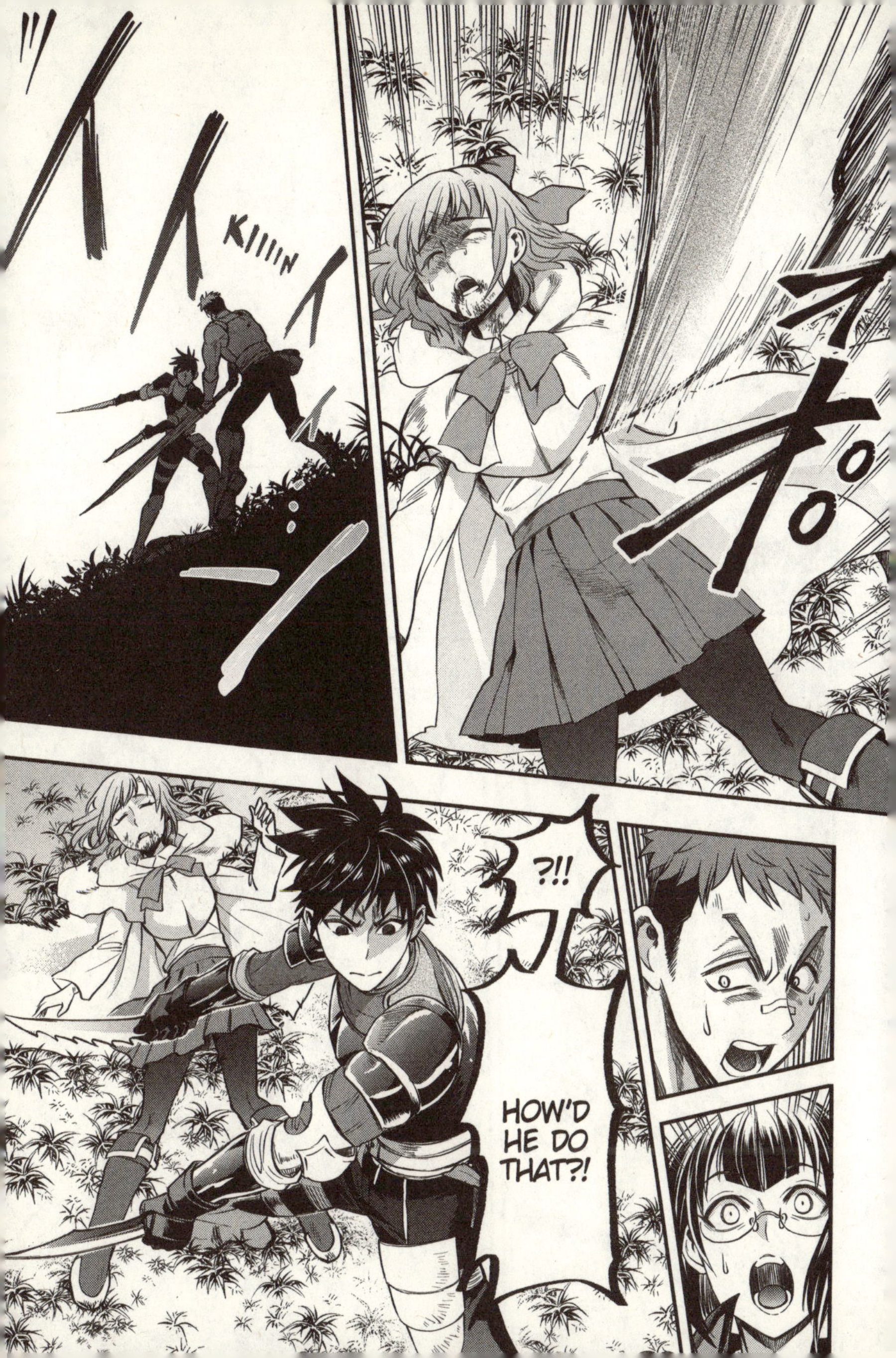
KIIIN
?!!
HOW'D HE DO THAT?!

MR. IN-VISIBLE?!
OOISO-SAN, TAKE KAREN!!
HURRY!!!
RUN!!
HAR-RIER!
SHOOT 'EM DEAD!!
GRIIK
BWSH

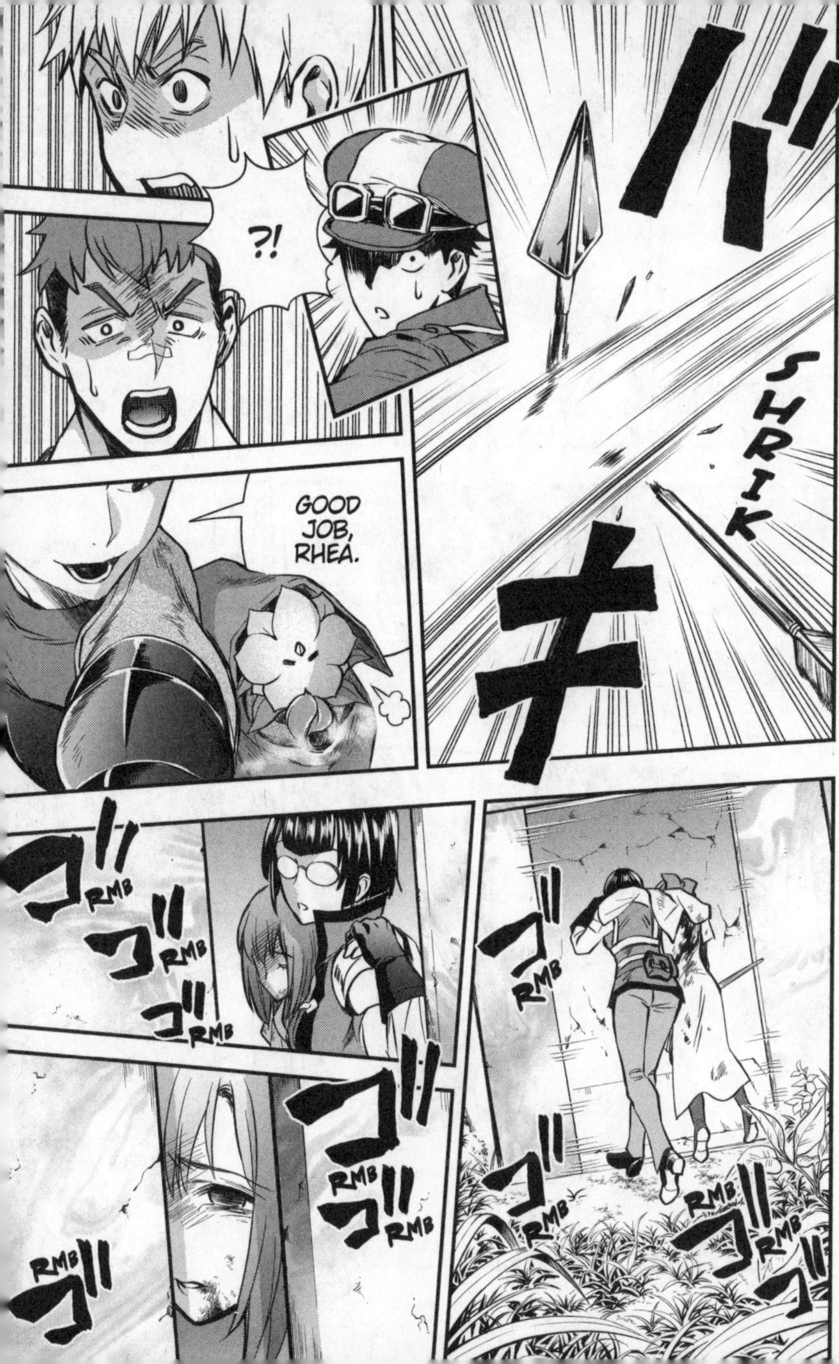
SHRIK
?!
GOOD JOB, RHEA.
RMB
RMB
RMB
RMB
RMB
RMB
RMB
RMB
RMB
RMB

GOOD.
GOOON
WHERE THE HELL'D HE GO?!
UH, I'M RIGHT IN FRONT OF YOU.
BLUNT
DO THEY HAVE ZERO DETECTION SKILLS?
SHOW YOURSELF, YOU FREAK!
GRIP
DAZE
FLINCH

H-HOW LONG HAVE YOU BEEN THERE?!
I'VE BEEN HERE...
THE WHOLE DAMN TIME!!
ONLY COWARDS HIDE IN BATTLE!!

HOW MANY TIMES DO YOU GOTTA GET IN OUR WAY UNTIL YOU'RE SATISFIED?!!
I WASN'T TRYING TO GET IN YOUR WAY LAST TIME.
GWAH HA!
GWAH HA!
MASATSUGU ISN'T HERE TO SAVE YOUR ASS!
HEH! QUIT ACTING TOUGH!!
TRUE.
BUT SO WHAT?
YOU'RE PRE-PARED...
TO DIE, AREN'T YOU?
A-ARE YOU FOR REAL?
C'MON, MAN. THIS WAS ALL A JOKE.
JAKIIN
A JOKE?

INJURING SOMEONE...
IS YOUR IDEA OF A JOKE?
LOOK, THAT WAS AN ACCI-DENT!
WE WON'T DO IT AGAIN! LET IT SLIDE, OKAY?
......
WAS TROLLING MY BLOG...
JUST A JOKE, TOO?
WH-WHAT DO YOU MEAN?
OUT OF THE TEN HATE COMMENTS I RECEIVED, THERE WERE SIX UNIQUE VISITORS.
Page views:14
Comments:10
Comment list
1: Anonymous user
2: Anonymous user
3: Anonymous user
4: Anonymous user
Die Die Die Die
THAT MEANS MY DAILY VIEWER COUNT ROSE BY THREE.
OR IN OTHER WORDS, THE SIZE OF YOUR PARTY.

IS YOUR BLOG THAT DEAD?
WE THOUGHT YOUR THANKFUL REPLIES WERE SARCASTIC, BUT HOLY SHIT, YOU WERE SERIOUS.
YOU'RE SO STARVED FOR COM-MENTS YOU'RE HAPPY TO GET TROLLED?
THAT'S JUST SAD...
DON'T GIVE ME THAT LOOK!
DAMMIT! I'M NEVER TALKING ABOUT MY BLOG AGAIN!
RMB RMB...
!
GWRRRM
RMB RMB
RMB
RMB
RMB
THIS FEELS FAMIL-IAR...
IS IT A MONSTER SWARM?!

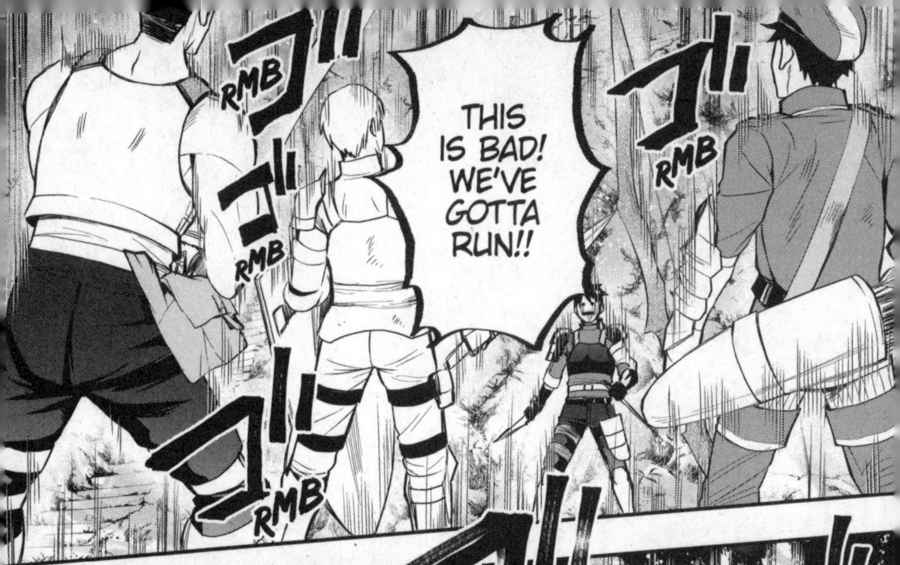
RMB
THIS IS BAD! WE'VE GOTTA RUN!!
RMB
RMB
RMB
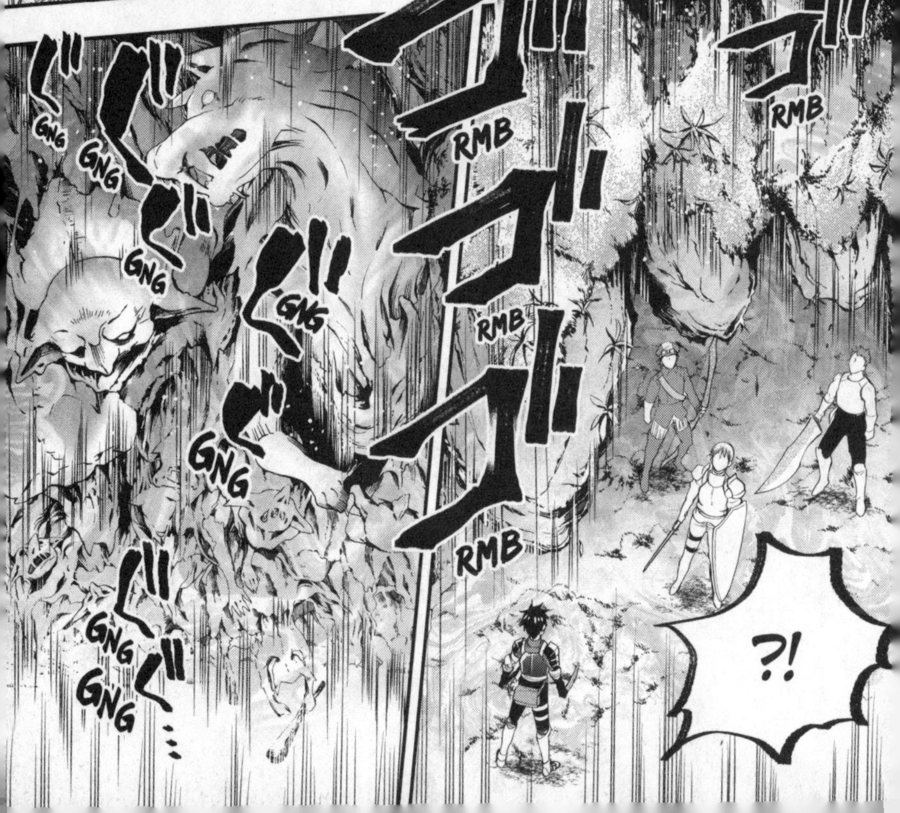
RMB
RMB
RMB
RMB
?!
GNG
GNG
GNG
GNG
GNG
GNG
GNG

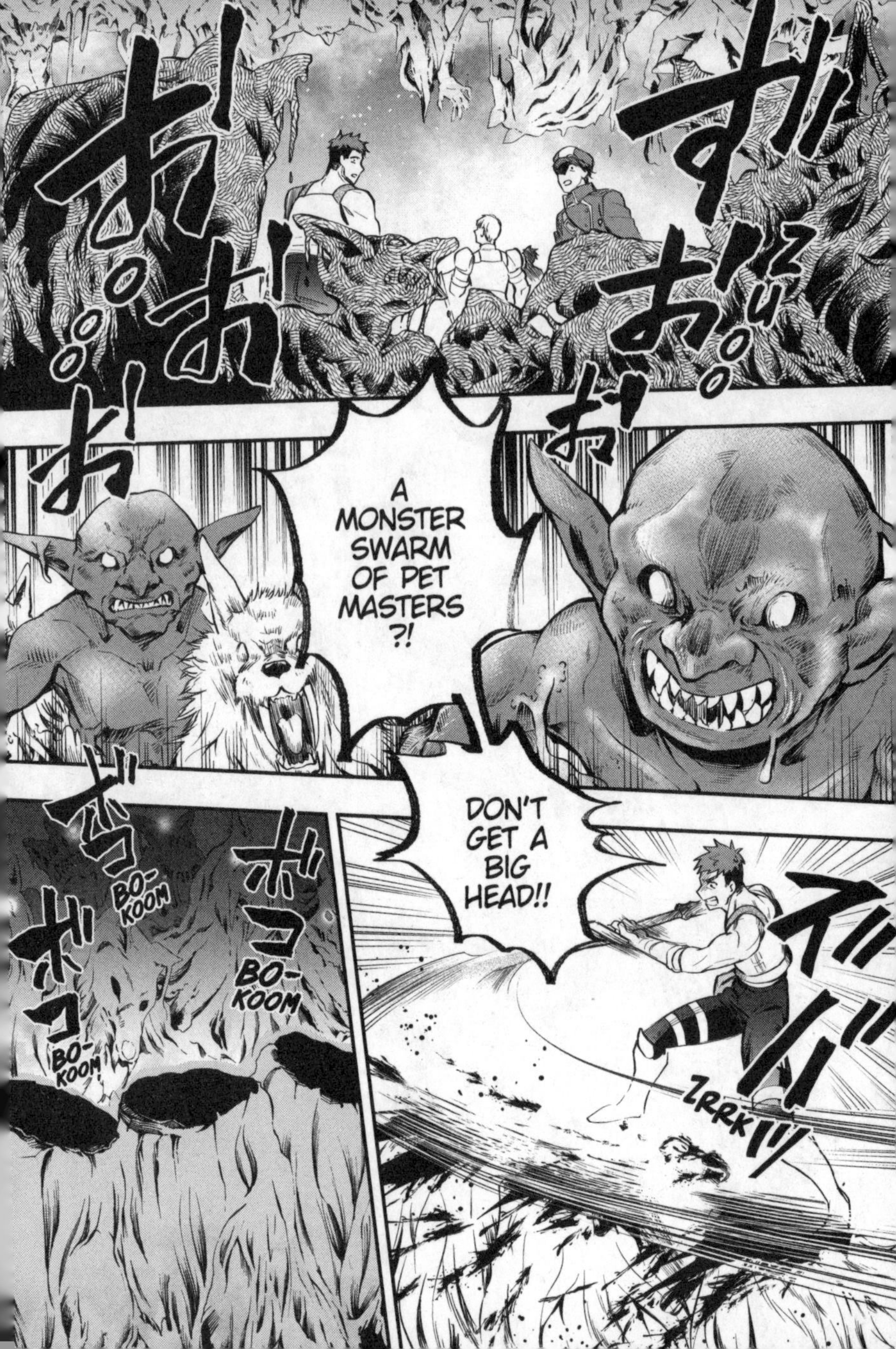
A MONSTER SWARM OF PET MASTERS?!
DON'T GET A BIG HEAD!!
ZRRK!!
BO-KOOM
BO-KOOM
BO-KOOM

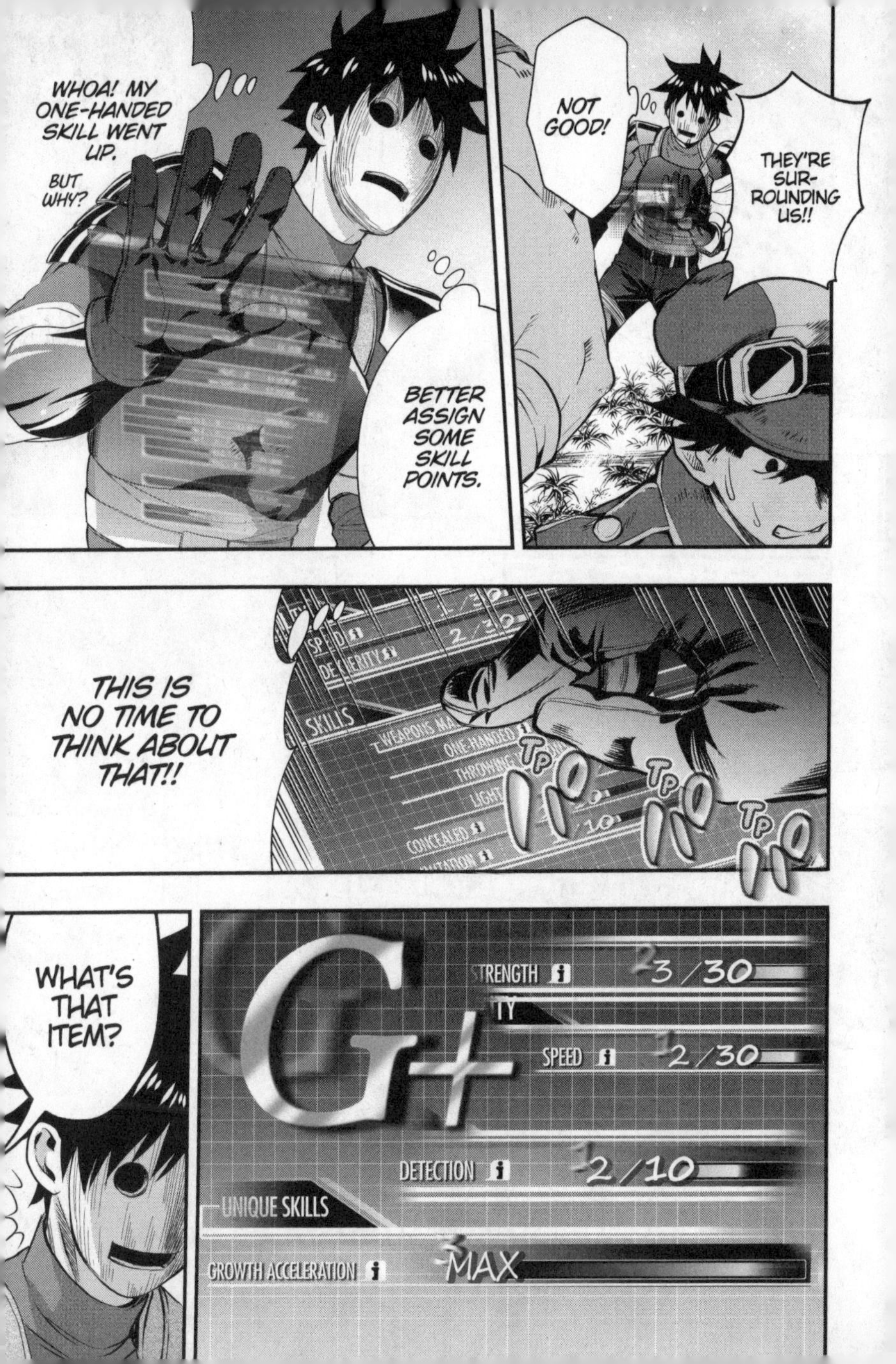

THEY'RE SUR-ROUNDING US!!
NOT GOOD!
WHOA! MY ONE-HANDED SKILL WENT UP.
BUT WHY?
BETTER ASSIGN SOME SKILL POINTS.
SPEED
DEXTERITY
SKILLS
ONE-HANDED
THROWING
CONCEALED
TP TP TP
THIS IS NO TIME TO THINK ABOUT THAT!!
G+
STRENGTH 3/30
SPEED 2/30
DETECTION 2/10
UNIQUE SKILLS
GROWTH ACCELERATION MAX
WHAT'S THAT ITEM?

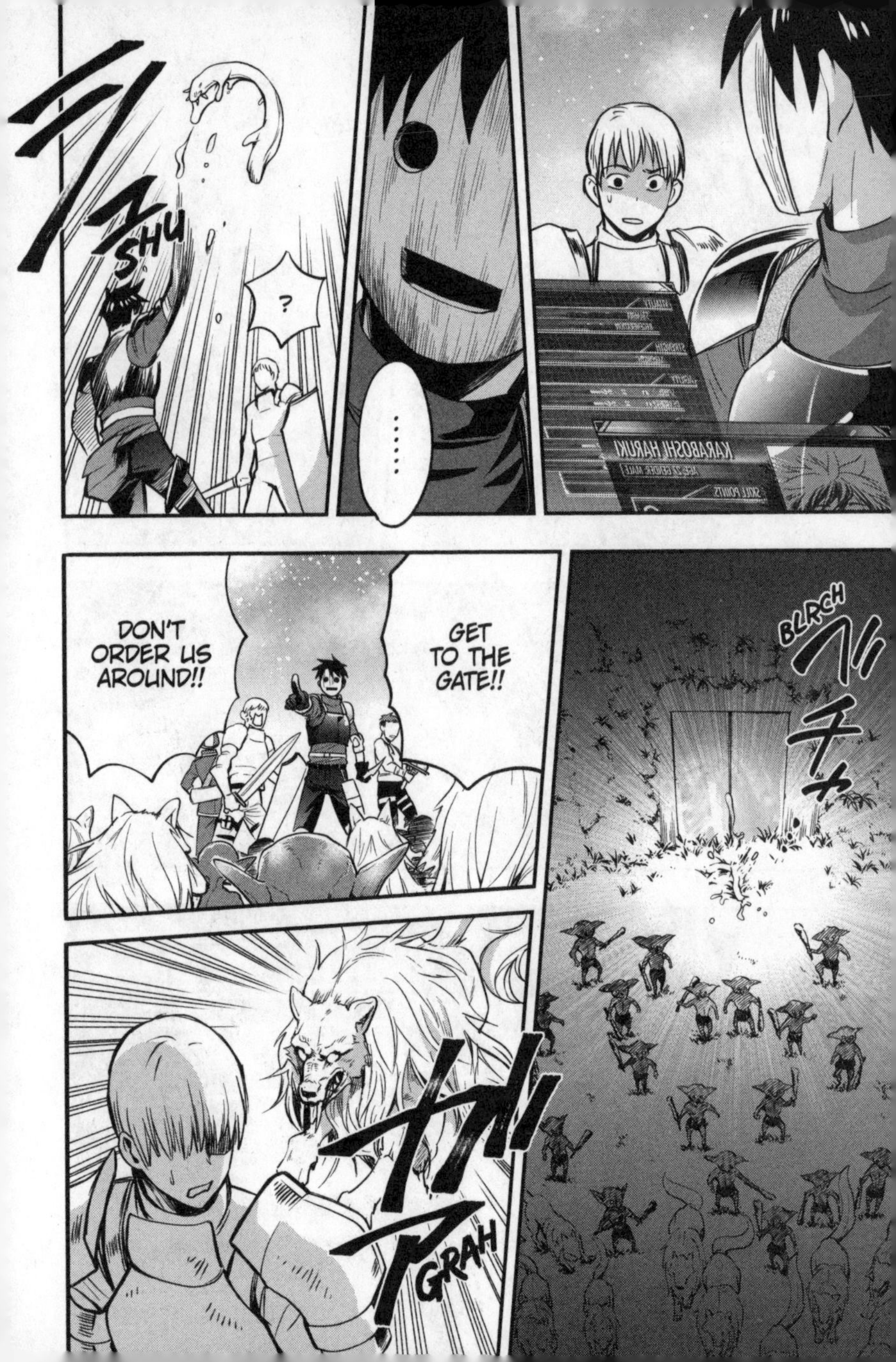
KARABOSHI HARUKI
SKILL POINTS
......
SHU
?
BLRCH
GET TO THE GATE!!
DON'T ORDER US AROUND!!
GRAH

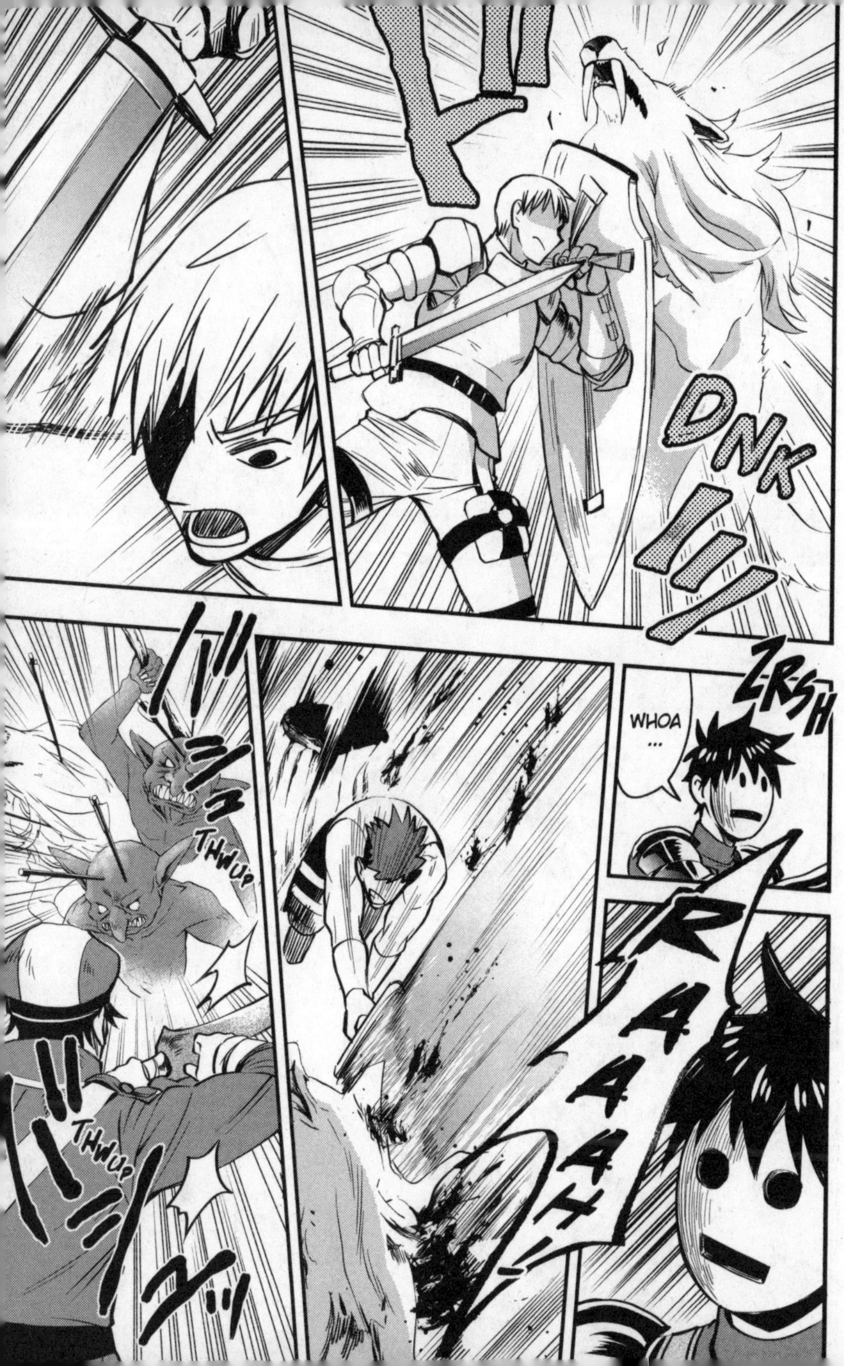

DNK
Z-R-SH
WHOA ...
RAAAAAH
THWUP
THWUP

SHOULD HAVE EXPECTED AS MUCH FROM ADVENTURERS WHO'VE CLEARED THE NINTH LEVEL.
THEIR COORDINATION IS ON POINT, AND THEIR STRENGTH IS NOTHING TO SCOFF AT.
WE CAN DO THIS!
WE'RE GONNA MAKE IT HOME SAFE!
CLENCH
QUIT ACTING LIKE OUR BOSS!!

HUH?!

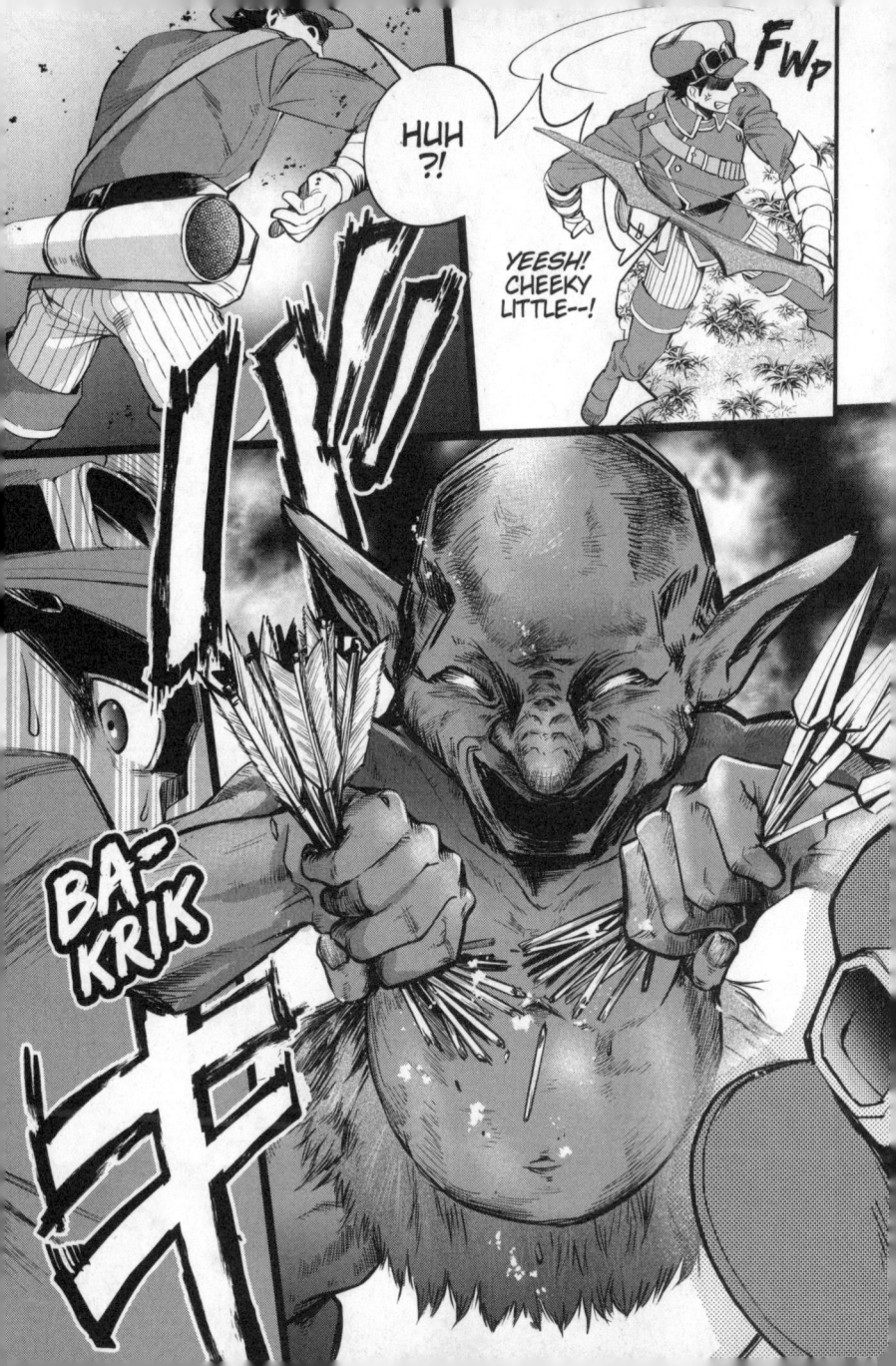

Fwp

YEESH! CHEEKY LITTLE--!

BA-KRIK

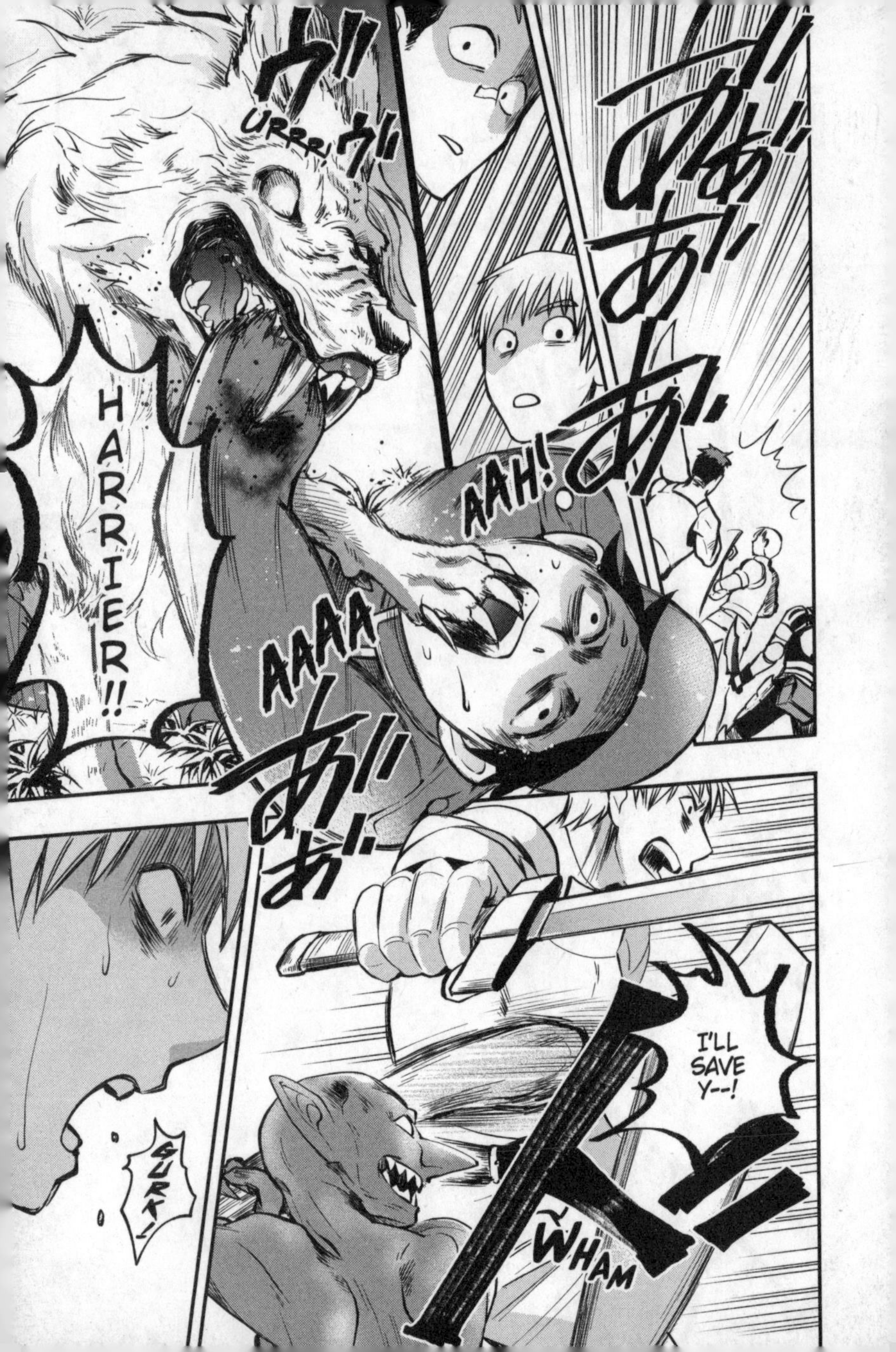

うゔ
URRR!
ゔ
HARRIER!!
ああああ
AAH!
ああ
AAAA
あああ
I'LL SAVE Y--!
GURK!
WHAM

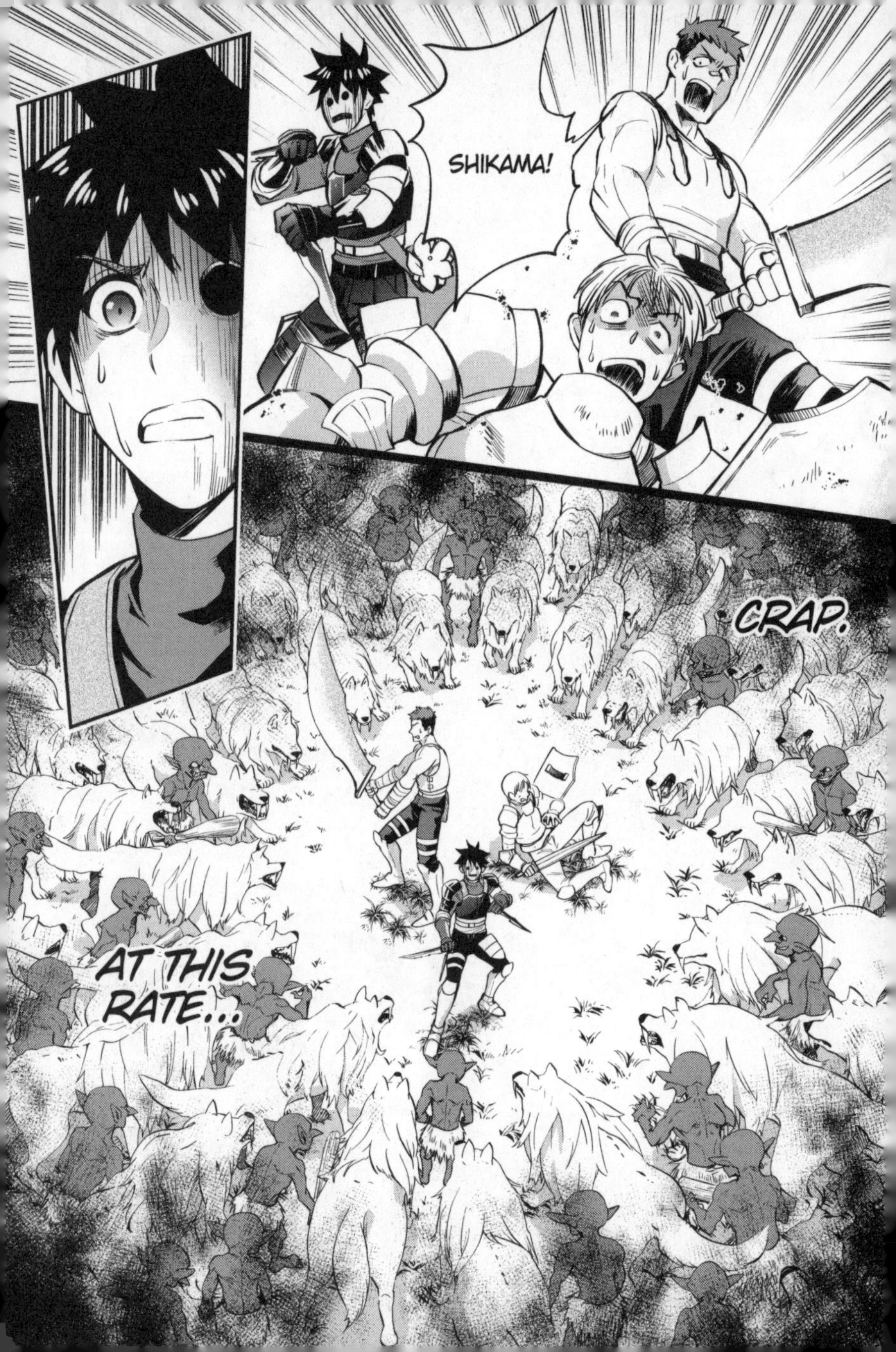
SHIKAMA!
CRAP.
AT THIS RATE...

CALL TO ADVENTURE!
DEFEATING DUNGEONS
WITH A SKILL BOARD

4

Chapter 17
HAR-RIER!
I'M COMING!
LEMME CUT A PATH OPEN!!
JUST HANG ON!
GRNK
GRNK
SCARF
......

DAMMIIIT!
WAIT! YOUR SWORD ISN'T ENOUGH TO--!
うおおおお
RAAAAAAAH!
GYAAAAAAH!
SHRIK
ZA

WHAT THE HELL ARE YOU DOING?!!
WE CAN'T BEAT THEM!!
DO
DO
OBVIOUSLY! AND NO ONE WOULD KNOWINGLY DIVE INTO A MONSTER SWARM!
BUT THIS IS DIFFER-ENT!
IF YOU DON'T FIGHT, YOU'LL DIE!!

WE CAN STILL SALVAGE THIS!
DON'T YOU WANT TO SAVE YOUR FRIEND?!
ZSH
ZSH
ぐわっ
GRAH!
SHUT THE HELL UP!!
IF IT WEREN'T FOR YOU--!
DUN
WE JUST NEED TO REACH THE GATE!

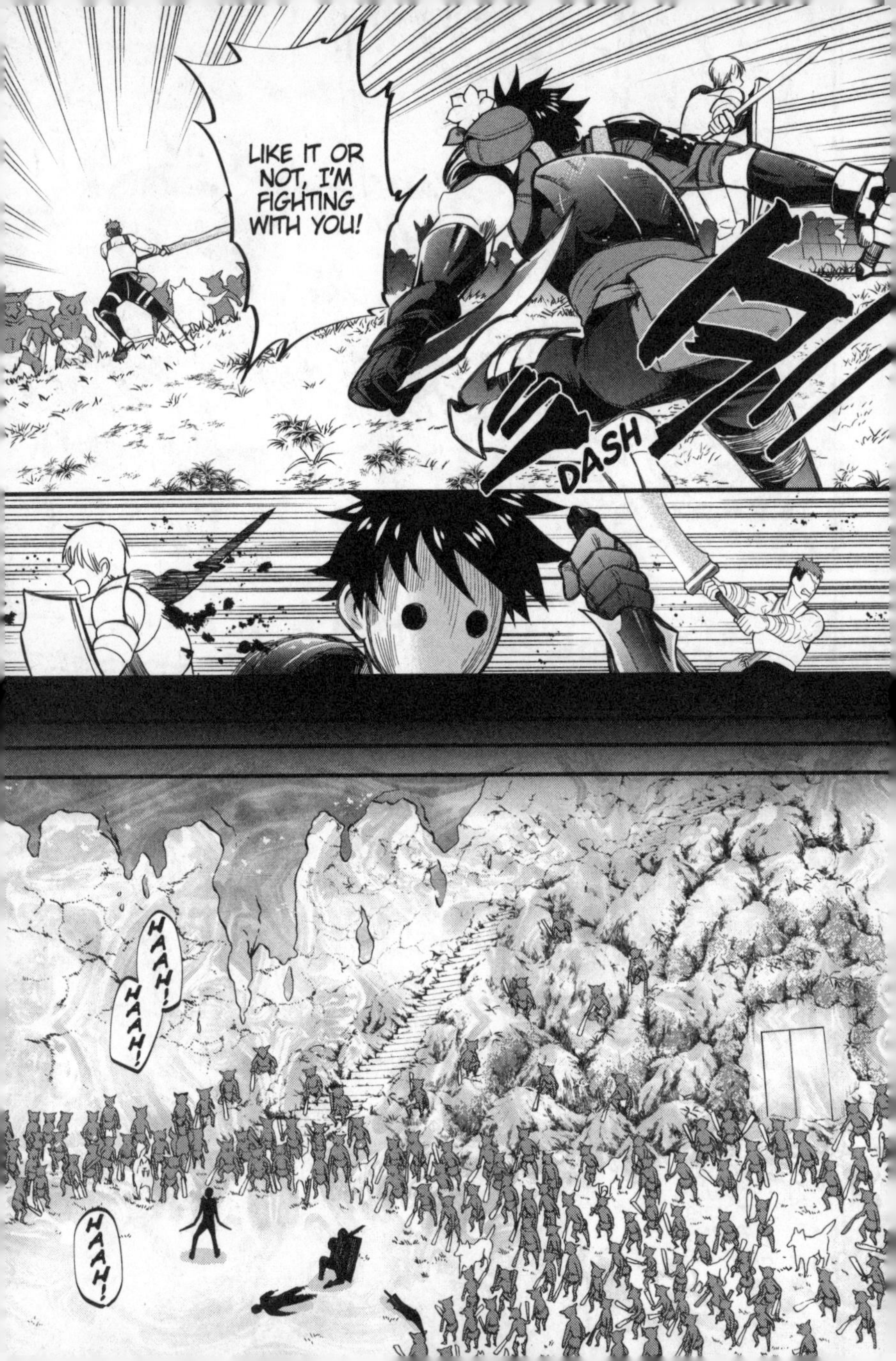
LIKE IT OR NOT, I'M FIGHTING WITH YOU!
DASH
HAAH! HAAH! HAAH!
HAAH!

HWEE!
HWEE!
THIS IS POINTLESS...
WE CAN'T... GET PAST THEM.
LANCE!
GWMP
WHAT THE HELL IS THIS?!
THEY KEEP COMING!
NO MATTER HOW MANY WE KILL!!
HE'S RIGHT!
ZRSH
WHY WON'T THIS END?!
WE'VE KILLED AT LEAST THREE HUNDRED!

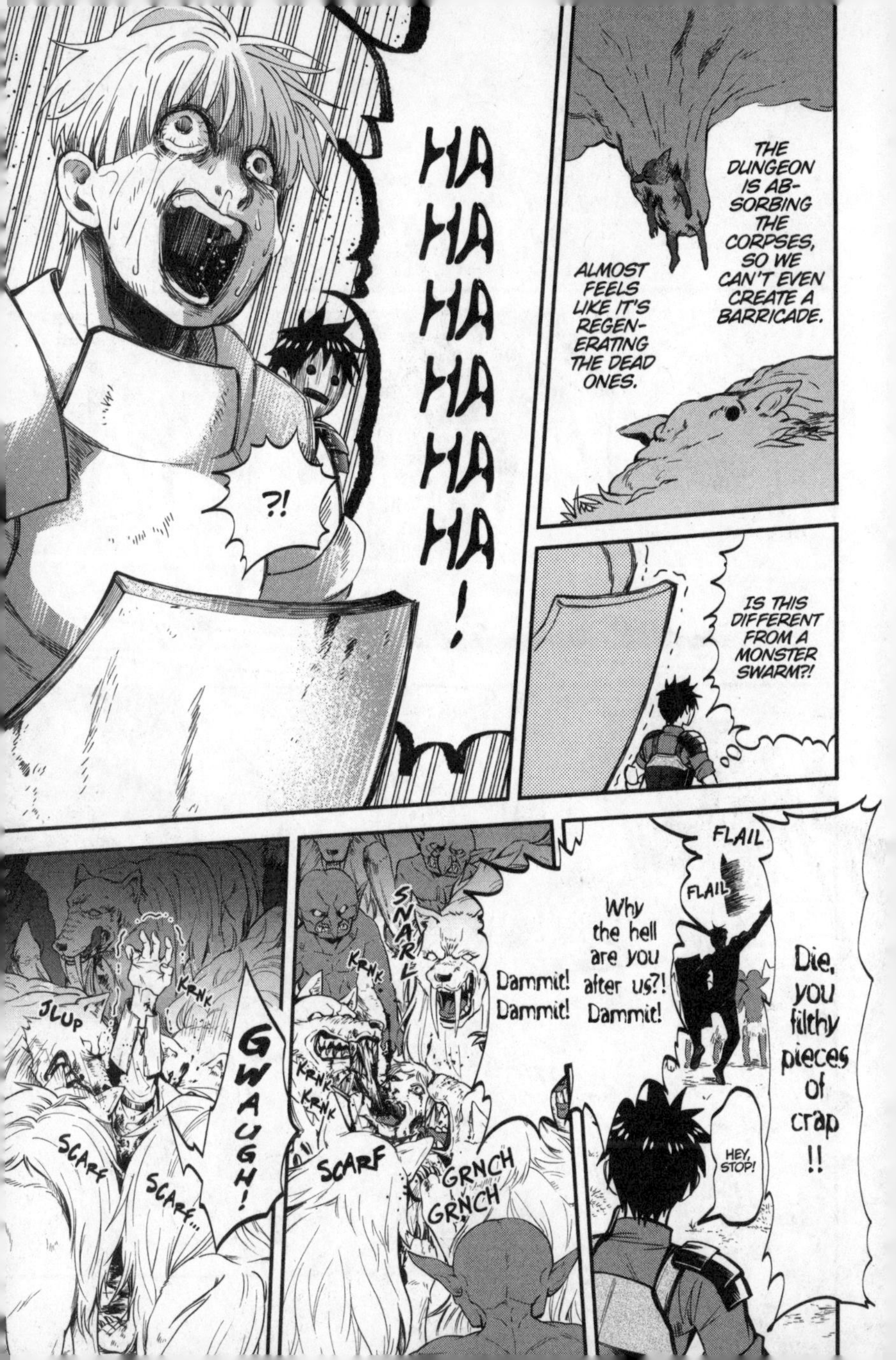

THE DUNGEON IS ABSORBING THE CORPSES, SO WE CAN'T EVEN CREATE A BARRICADE.
ALMOST FEELS LIKE IT'S REGENERATING THE DEAD ONES.
IS THIS DIFFERENT FROM A MONSTER SWARM?!
HA HA HA HA HA HA!
?!
FLAIL
FLAIL
Die, you filthy pieces of crap!!
Why the hell are you after us?! Dammit!
Dammit! Dammit!
HEY, STOP!
SNARL
KRNK
KRNK
KRNK
SCARF
GRNCH GRNCH
JLUP
KRNK
GWAUGH!
SCARF
SCARF...

"...!"

RHEA...

WE'RE GONNA RAM OUR WAY THROUGH!

SURE, THIS ISN'T A NORMAL MONSTER SWARM...

BUT THERE HAS TO BE A CENTER POINT!

SOUND IT OUT.

LOOK CLOSELY.

WHAT'S THAT?!

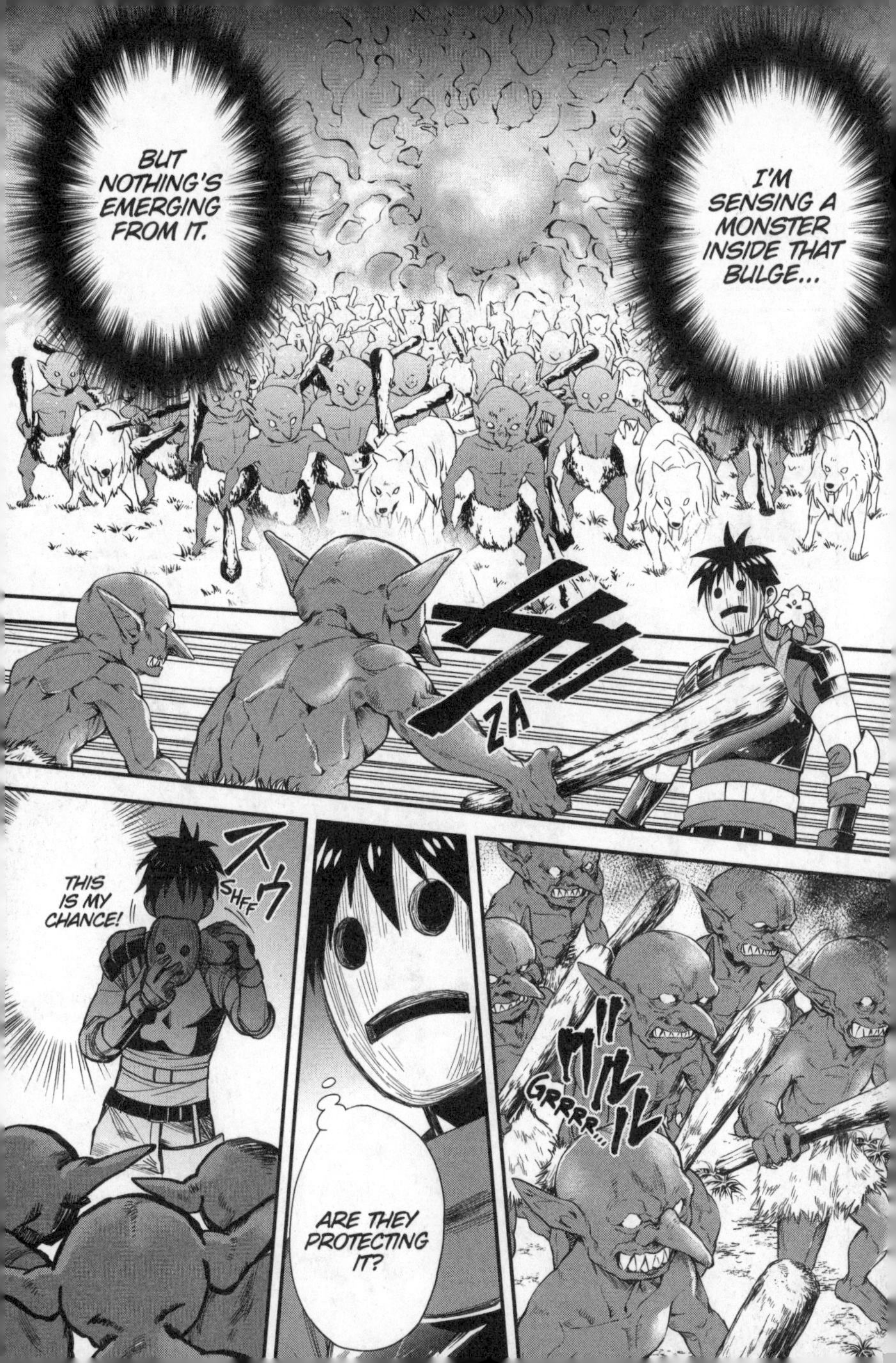

I'M SENSING A MONSTER INSIDE THAT BULGE...
BUT NOTHING'S EMERGING FROM IT.
ZA
GRRRR...
ARE THEY PROTECTING IT?
SHFF
THIS IS MY CHANCE!

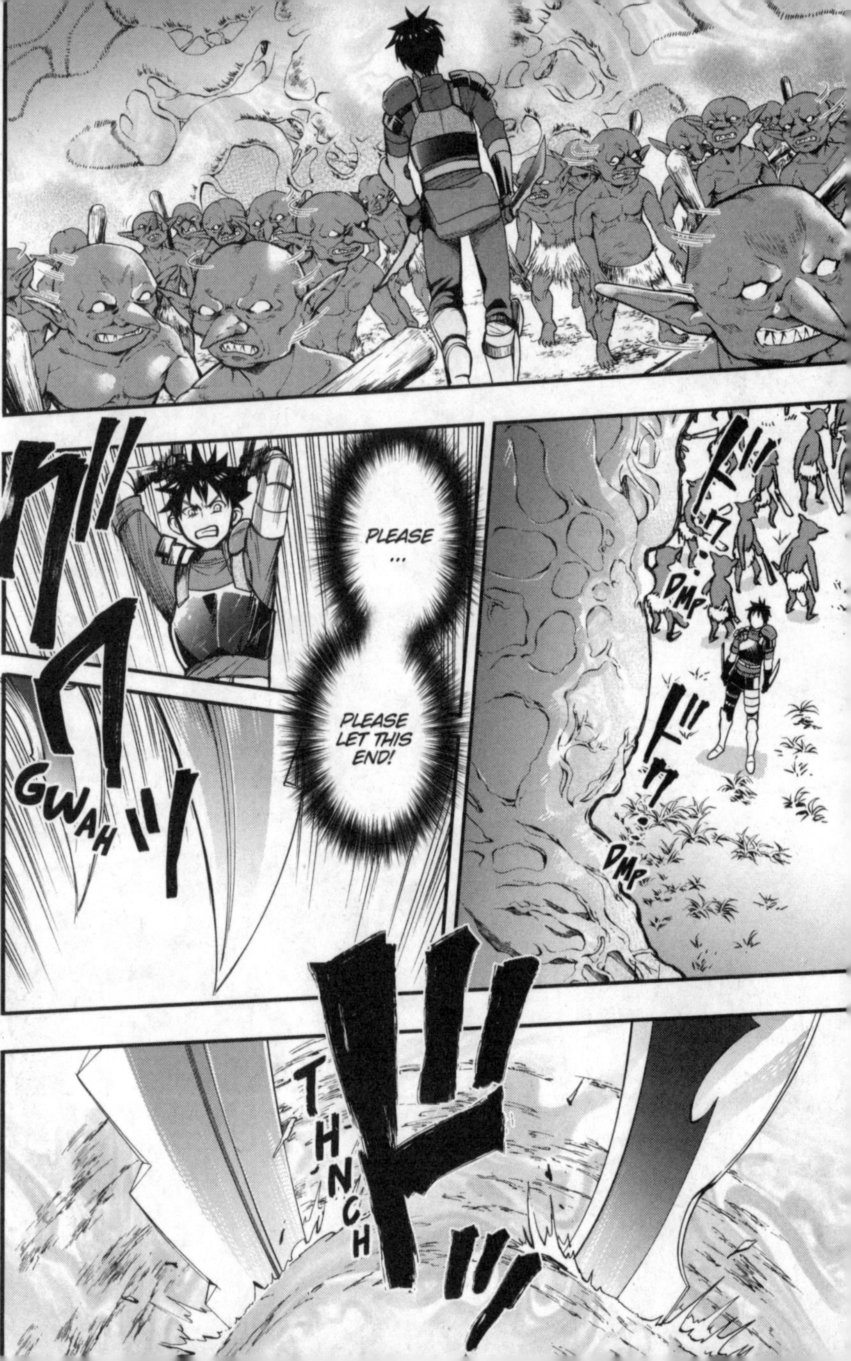
DMP
DMP
PLEASE ...
PLEASE LET THIS END!
GWAH
THNCH

ZUBA

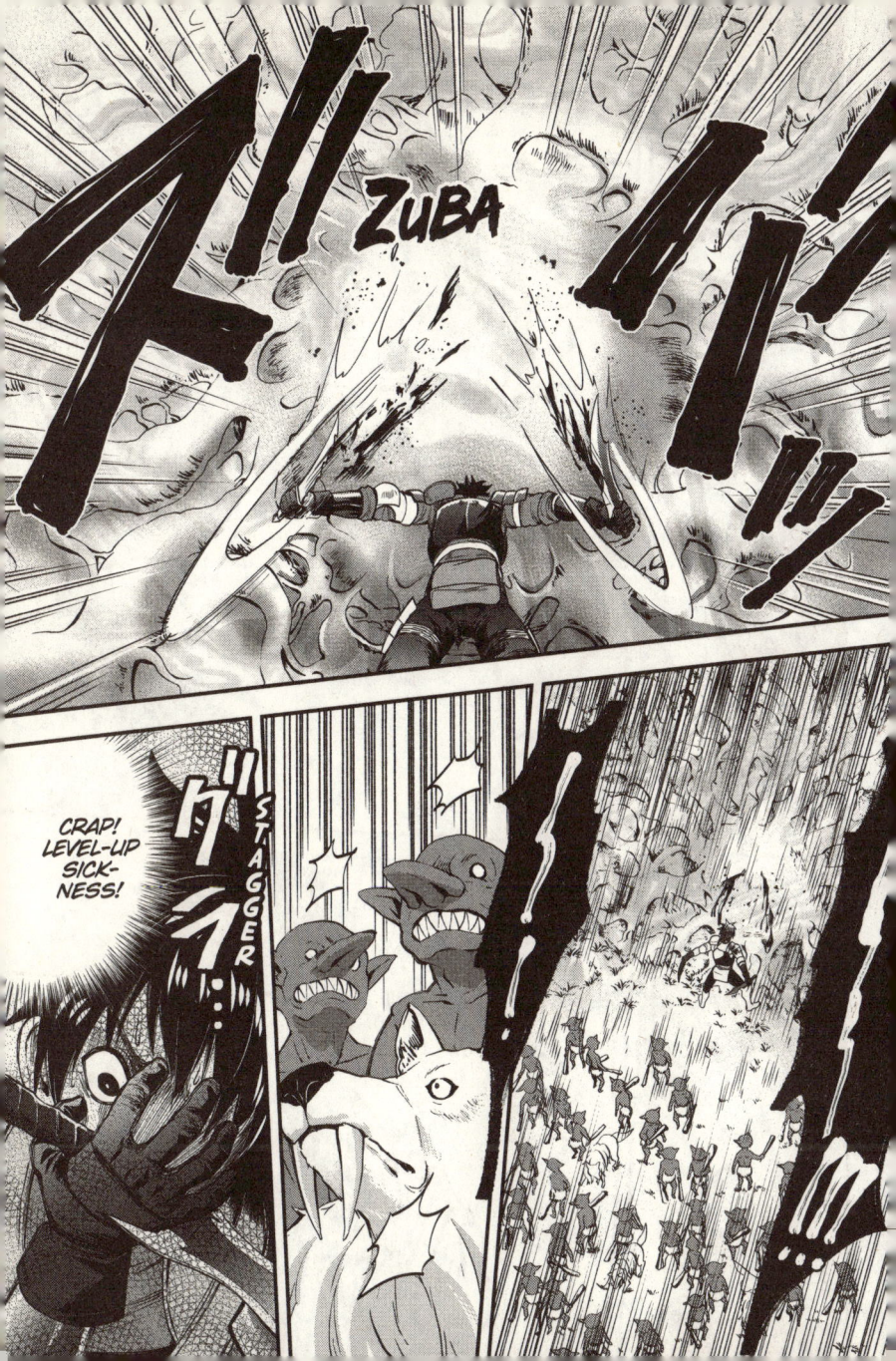

CRAP! LEVEL-UP SICKNESS!

STAGGER

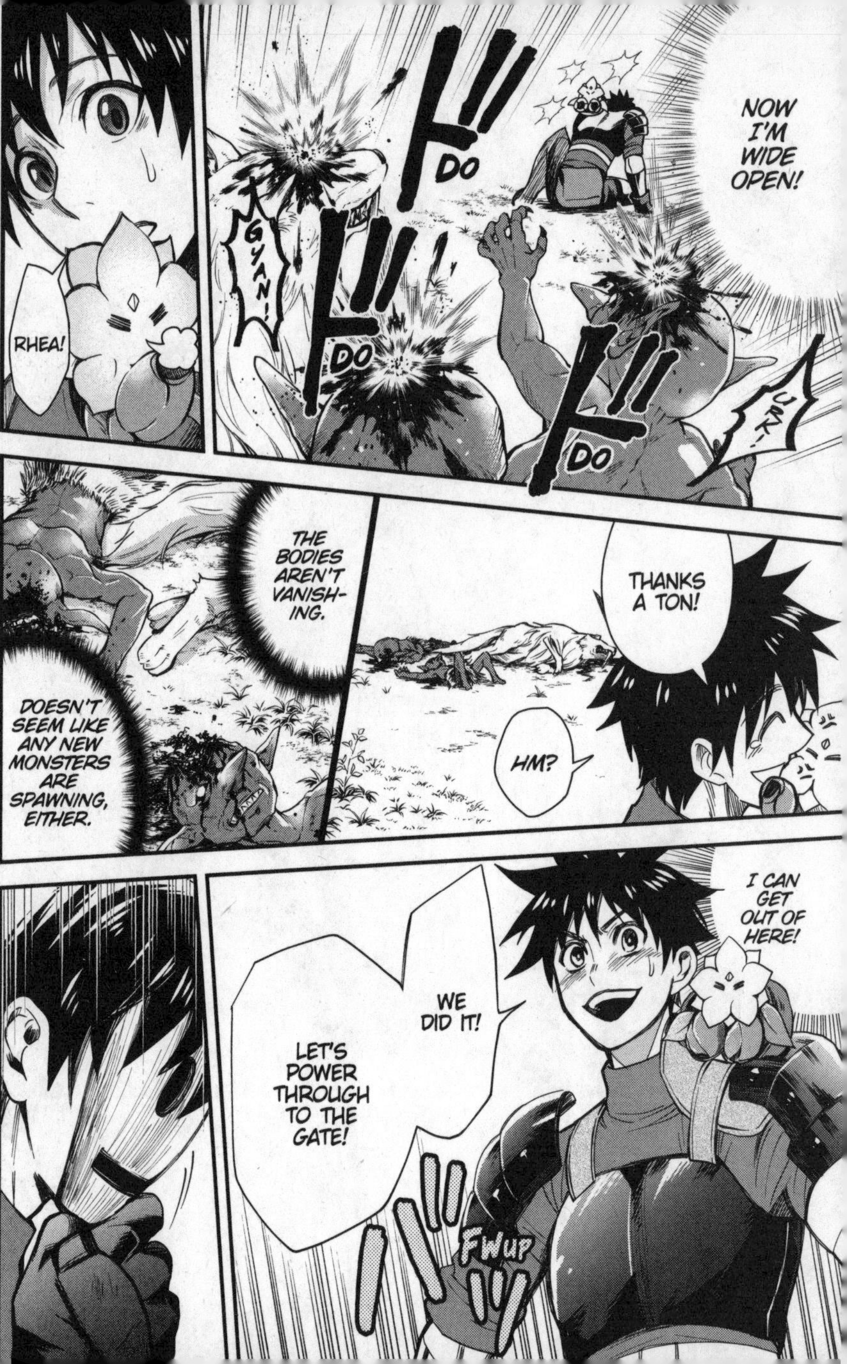
NOW I'M WIDE OPEN!
DO
GYAN!
DO
DO
URK!
RHEA!
THANKS A TON!
HM?
THE BODIES AREN'T VANISHING.
DOESN'T SEEM LIKE ANY NEW MONSTERS ARE SPAWNING, EITHER.
I CAN GET OUT OF HERE!
WE DID IT!
LET'S POWER THROUGH TO THE GATE!
FWUP

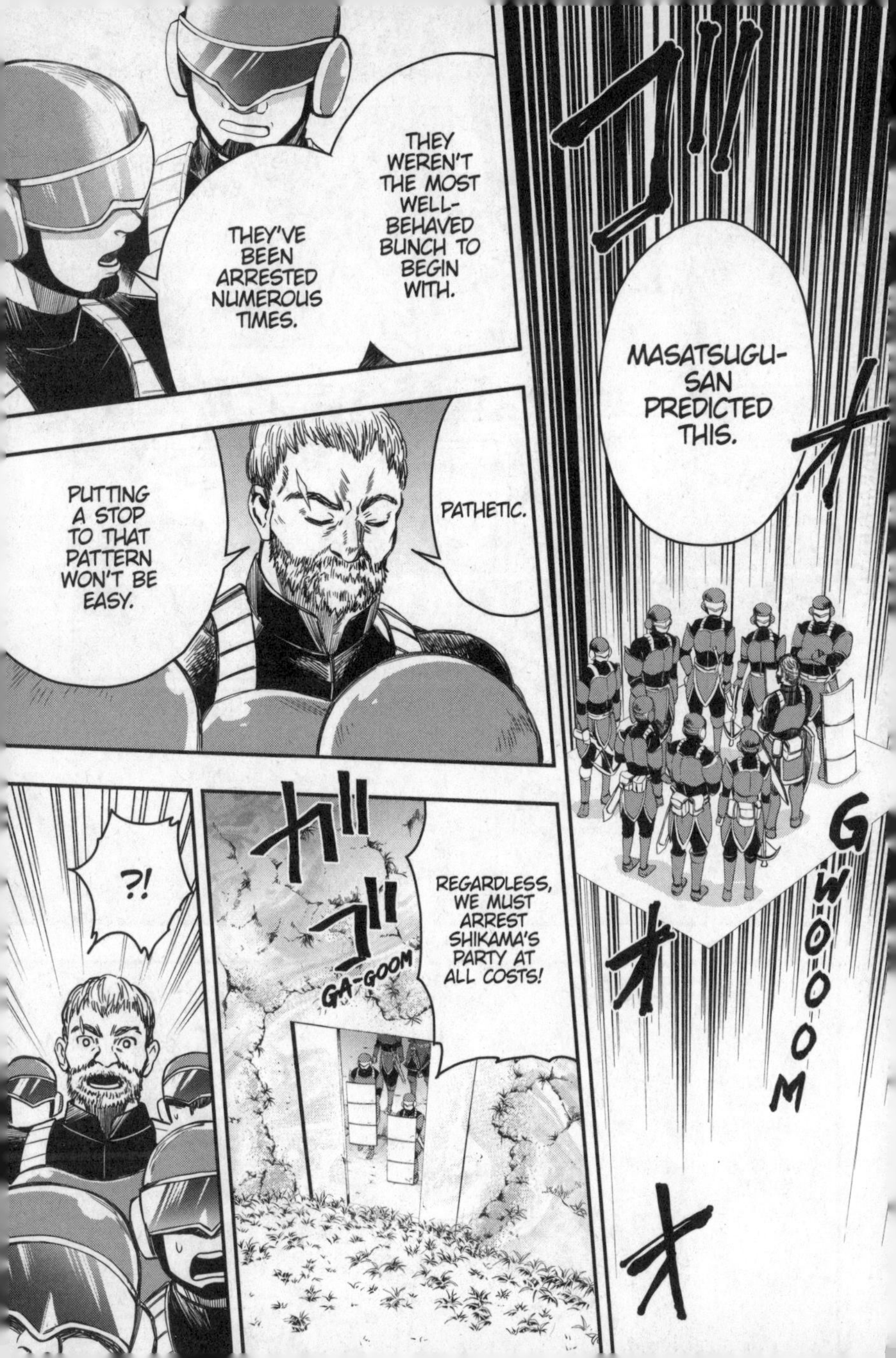
MASATSUGU-SAN PREDICTED THIS.
GWOOOOM
THEY WEREN'T THE MOST WELL-BEHAVED BUNCH TO BEGIN WITH.
THEY'VE BEEN ARRESTED NUMEROUS TIMES.
PATHETIC.
PUTTING A STOP TO THAT PATTERN WON'T BE EASY.
GA-GOOM
REGARDLESS, WE MUST ARREST SHIKAMA'S PARTY AT ALL COSTS!
?!

A MONSTER SWARM?!
DO
DO
DO
READY YOUR CROSS-BOWS!!
DUN
SHAK
SHAK
WAIT!
WE'RE OVER HERE!!
WHAT IS THAT?
A PLANT AND A MASK?
WHY ARE THEY FLOATING?
IS IT A MON-STER?
I'M MR. INVISIBLE, AN ADVEN-TURER! THANKS FOR HELPING OUT!!

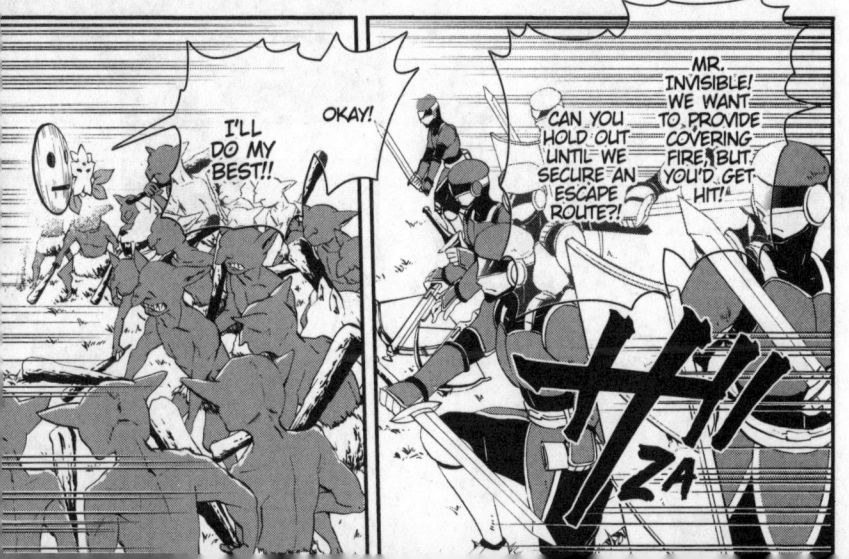

"I COULDN'T SAVE THEM!"

"ADVENTURER MR. INVISIBLE! WHAT HAPPENED TO SHIKAMA'S PARTY?!"

"IS HE A MEMBER OF SHIKAMA'S PARTY?"

"WH-WHAT DO WE DO, COMMANDER?"

"COMMANDER, LOOK."

"MR. INVISIBLE! WE WANT TO PROVIDE COVERING FIRE, BUT YOU'D GET HIT!"

"CAN YOU HOLD OUT UNTIL WE SECURE AN ESCAPE ROUTE?!"

"OKAY!"

"I'LL DO MY BEST!!"

ALL UNITS, USE CLOSE-RANGE WEAPONS AND PRIORITIZE RESCUE!!
YES, SIR!
A SLIMY EEL?
DWMP
WHOA!
YOU SURE HAULED ASS!
GOOD!
MAINTAIN FORMATION AND RETREAT!
YES, SIR!

GA-KOOM
HEY, WHY DO YOU USE A SHORT SWORD?
IS THAT MASK A MAGIC TOOL?
DOES IT IMPROVE YOUR PHYSICAL ABILITIES?
IS THAT PLANT A MONSTER?
IT'S SUPER CUTE!
SHE IS. I TAMED HER.
T-T-TAMED?!!
ARE YOU SERIOUS?!!
QUIT MAKING A RUCKUS! YOU CAN ASK ALL THE QUESTIONS YOU WANT ONCE WE'RE TOPSIDE!
BUT!
HE'S THE FIRST HUMAN TO TAME ONE!
C'MON!
SHF SHF
HOW ODD.
AT A GLANCE, HIS ABILITIES SEEM AVER-AGE...
YET HE CALMLY DEALT WITH A MONSTER SWARM...
AND TAMED A MONSTER TO BOOT.

WAIT, I REMEMBER YOU! YOU'RE THAT ADVENTURER FROM THE RUMORS!
OH? IS HE FAMOUS?
FA-MOUS ?!!
MASATSUGU-SAN KNOWS THIS GUY.
PEOPLE SAY HE'S CLOSING IN ON THE RANKERS.
THE MASKED PERVERT !!!
?!
BA-
TNK

Ichibishi Armor Shop
Ichibishi Buyouts
NOD
HOW IS KAREN DOING?
NOD
JOLT
AH!
M-MR. INVISIBLE, RIGHT? I'M SORRY.
IT'S OKAY. I KNOW YOU MUST BE TIRED.
THANKS FOR LOOKING AFTER KAREN.
THIS IS NOTHING COMPARED TO WHAT I OWE YOU.
NGH...

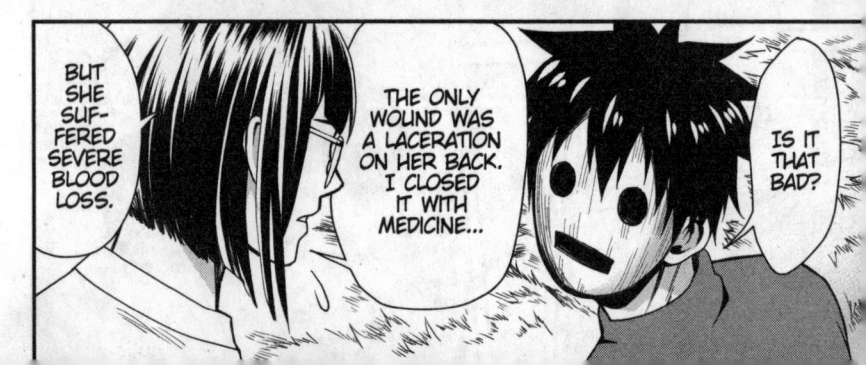

KARA-BOSHI-SAN?

...

KAREN.

...

UNGH...

HUH?! ARE YOU OKAY?!

DON'T MAKE ANY SUDDEN MOVEMENTS!

FWMP

SWAY

FWUP

!

KARA-BOSHI-SAN!!

BUT SHE SUFFERED SEVERE BLOOD LOSS.

THE ONLY WOUND WAS A LACERATION ON HER BACK. I CLOSED IT WITH MEDICINE...

IS IT THAT BAD?

LUCKILY, HER ARMOR TOOK THE BRUNT OF THE ATTACK.

THANKS TO THAT, SHE'LL BE FINE SOON.

INCIDENTALLY...

I'M IMPRESSED YOU MANAGED TO SURVIVE THE SWARM.

THE POLICE TOLD ME ALL ABOUT IT BEFORE YOU ARRIVED.

THEY SAID YOU WERE AMAZING!

...

NO...

DON'T BLAME YOURSELF.
THEY GOT WHAT WAS COMING TO THEM.
EVERYTHING THAT HAPPENED... WAS KARMA FOR THEIR BEHAVIOR.
THE SAME GOES FOR ME, REALLY.
YOU SHOULD STAND PROUD.
UNDERSTAND?
...
THANK YOU.
CLENCH

THIS IS ALL MY FAULT.
IF I HADN'T TAKEN THAT HIT...
I'LL NEVER FORGIVE THEM FOR WHAT THEY DID.
BUT IF I HADN'T LET MY GUARD DOWN, MAYBE THEY ALL COULD'VE GOTTEN OUT ALIVE.
IF ONLY THAT WAS HOW IT ACTUALLY WENT DOWN.
THAT WAY, KARABOSHI-SAN WOULDN'T FEEL...
RESPONSIBLE FOR ALL THOSE LOST LIVES!

I'M SO SORRY!

KARA-BOSHI-SAN!

I'M SORRY FOR BEING SO PATHETIC!

IT'S ALL MY FAULT!

WHY THE APOLOGY?

...

IF I HADN'T BEEN THERE...

THIS NEVER WOULD'VE--

OWW!!

GONK

YOUR WARNING'S A LITTLE LATE!
GRRN
GRRN
GRRN
GRRN
GRRN
QUIT SPOUTING GARBAGE.
I'LL SMACK YOU.
A KARATE CHOP DOESN'T COUNT AS SMACKING.
THEY BROUGHT THIS UPON THEM-SELVES.
IT'S DEAD WRONG TO THINK THIS WAS YOUR FAULT.
I MEAN, I LET MY GUARD DOWN, TOO.
YOU GOT INJURED BECAUSE I WASN'T WATCHING FOR ENEMIES.
THAT'S MY BAD.
I'M SORRY.
YOU'RE WRONG! I WAS THE REAR GUARD, SO I SHOULD'VE--!
I SHOULD'VE BEEN STRONGER!!!

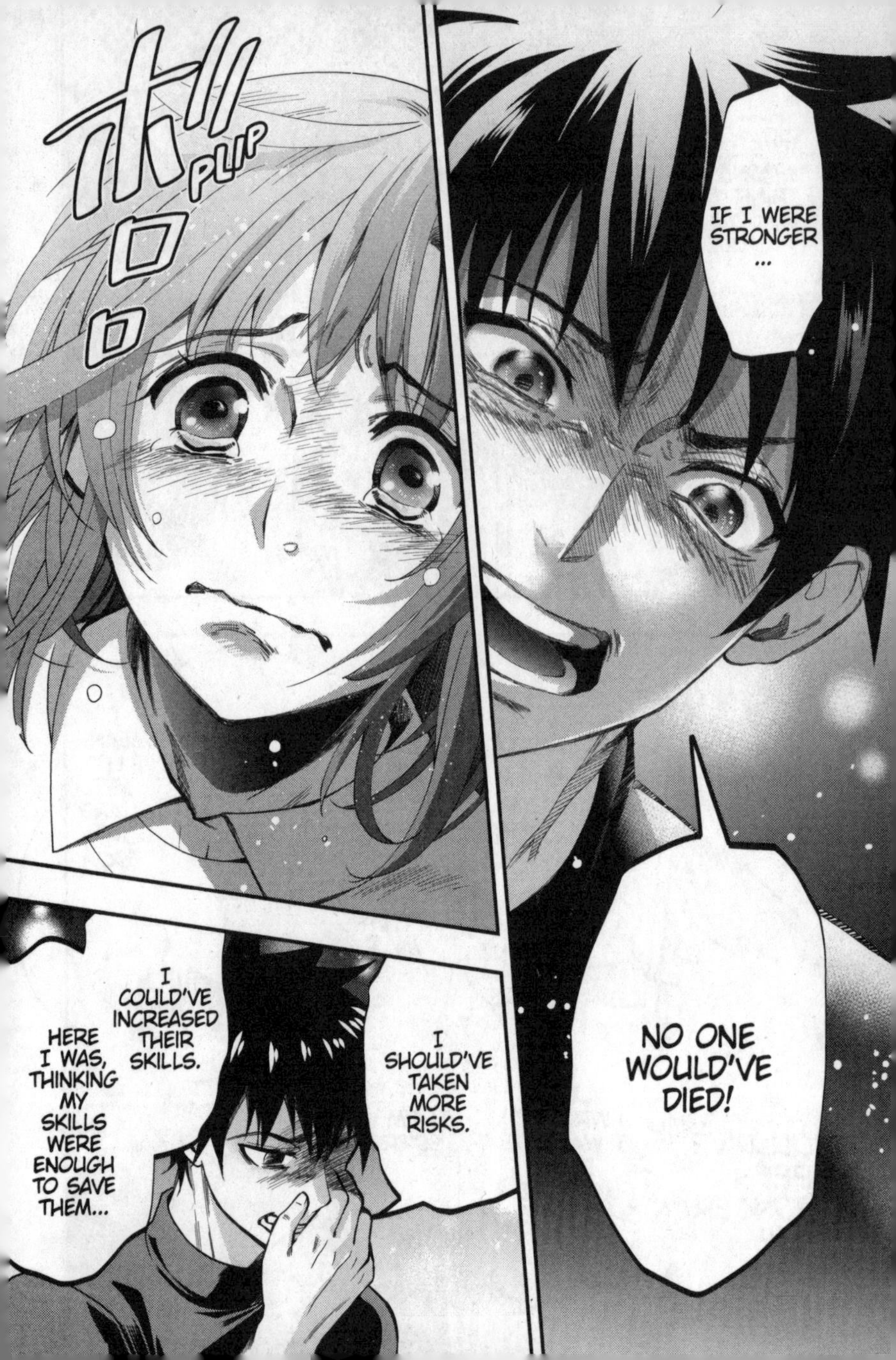
IF I WERE STRONGER ...
NO ONE WOULD'VE DIED!
PLIP
I SHOULD'VE TAKEN MORE RISKS.
I COULD'VE INCREASED THEIR SKILLS.
HERE I WAS, THINKING MY SKILLS WERE ENOUGH TO SAVE THEM...

BUT I DIDN'T DO ANYTHING TO HELP.
ALL I DID WAS LOOK AFTER MYSELF.
SHF..
LET'S GET STRONGER.
TOGETH-ER.
YEAH!

【 We found her! 】

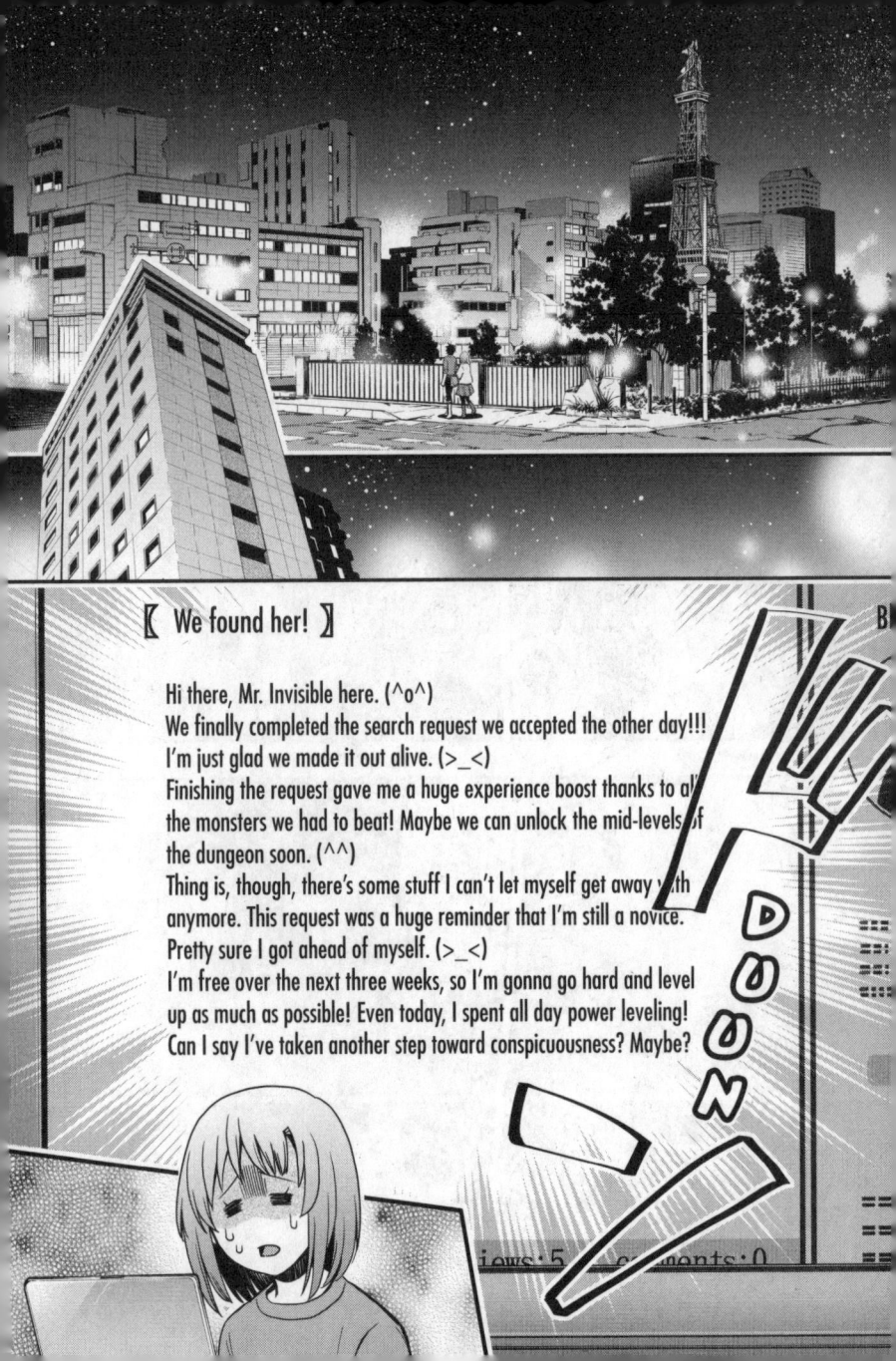

Hi there, Mr. Invisible here. (^o^)
We finally completed the search request we accepted the other day!!!
I'm just glad we made it out alive. (>_<)
Finishing the request gave me a huge experience boost thanks to all the monsters we had to beat! Maybe we can unlock the mid-levels of the dungeon soon. (^^)
Thing is, though, there's some stuff I can't let myself get away with anymore. This request was a huge reminder that I'm still a novice. Pretty sure I got ahead of myself. (>_<)
I'm free over the next three weeks, so I'm gonna go hard and level up as much as possible! Even today, I spent all day power leveling! Can I say I've taken another step toward conspicuousness? Maybe?

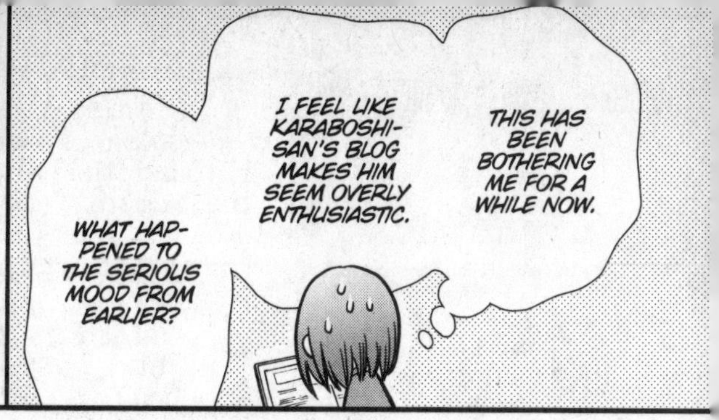
THIS HAS BEEN BOTHERING ME FOR A WHILE NOW.
I FEEL LIKE KARABOSHI-SAN'S BLOG MAKES HIM SEEM OVERLY ENTHUSIASTIC.
WHAT HAP-PENED TO THE SERIOUS MOOD FROM EARLIER?
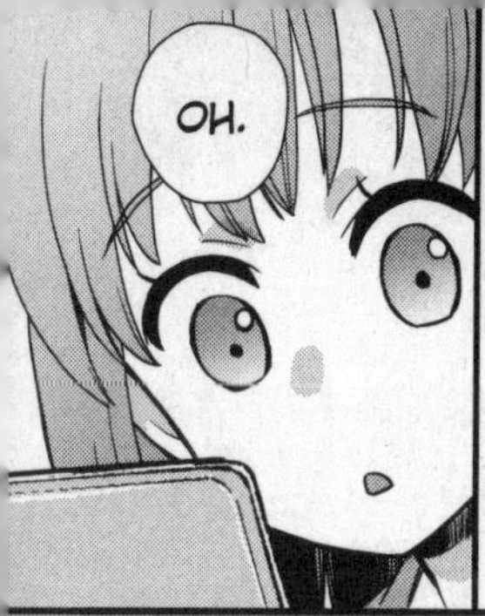
OH.
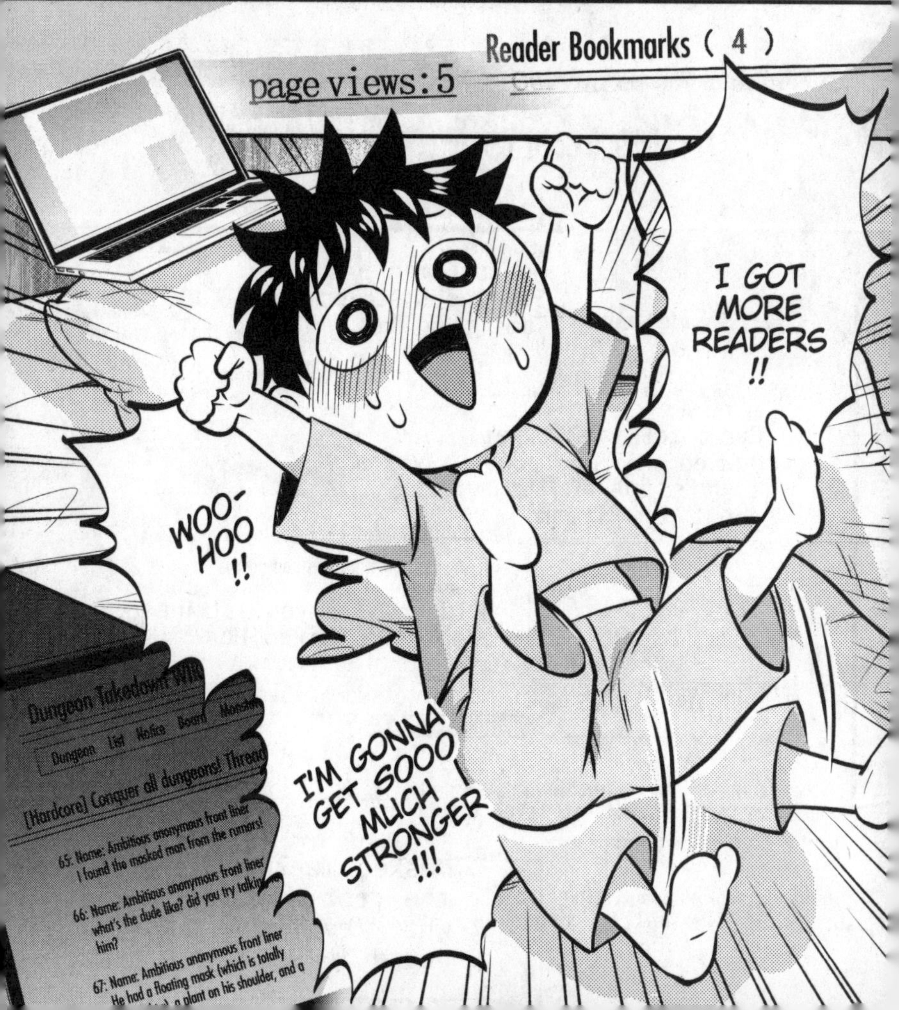
Reader Bookmarks (4)
page views: 5
I GOT MORE READERS !!
WOO-HOO !!
I'M GONNA GET SOOO MUCH STRONGER !!!
Dungeon List Notice Board
[Hardcore] Conquer all dungeons!
65: Name: Ambitious anonymous front liner
I found the masked man from the rumors!
66: Name: Ambitious anonymous front liner
what's the dude like? did you try
him?
67: Name: Ambitious anonymous front liner
He had a floating mask (which is totally
a plant on his shoulder, and a

[Hardcore] Traverse dungeons with

65: Name: Ambitious anonymous front liner
I found the masked man from the rumors!

66: Name: Ambitious anonymous front
what's the dude like? did you try tal

67: Name: Ambitious anonymous front liner
He had a floating mask (which is totally cursed, btw), a plant on his shoulder, and a tentacle on his arm.

68: Name: Ambitious anonymous front liner
Why's he keeping a monster?

[Casual] Chikaho discussion thread 70 [We're alive!]

110: Anonymous casual adventurer at Chikaho
Hot off the presses: Someone discovered a Taming skill!

111: Anonymous casu at Chikaho
no way! deets!!!

aho
wanna go public?

115: Anonymous casual adventurer at Chikaho
Can't tell. He'll get doxxed. All I'm gonna say is he's got a wild aura about him. Freaky

116: Anonymous casual adventurer at Chikaho
Hold on. Are you talking about the Masked Man?

[Elite] Monster swarm discussion

21: Real-life
Chikaho h

swarm killer
the masked man took out half of them and sent the rest running

l-life monster swarm killer
masked man? half? sent the rest running?
what level was that?
heard it was level ten

24: Real-life monster swarm killer
wasn't it level eight?

25: Real-life monster swarm killer
uh...what the hell?

CALL TO ADVENTURE!
DEFEATING DUN GEONS
WITH A SKILL BOARD

4

SOMETHING CRAZY HAPPENED.

Chapter 18

NEW KICKOFF 1/10
CONCEALED 2/10
IMITATION 2/10
LIGHT ARMOR 3/10

I'M IN POSSESSION... OF A NEW SECRET!

I'VE BEEN POWER LEVELING FOR THREE WEEKS SINCE THE SEARCH, AND THIS IS WHAT I GET?!!
I KNOW I SAID I WANTED TO GET STRONGER, BUT STILL!
OH.
HM?
MY ABILITIES IN-CREASED!
BUT YOU DIDN'T USE THE SKILL BOARD ON ME.
YOU MUST'VE IMPROVED NATURALLY.
YOU MENTIONED YOU'D BEEN WORKING OUT, RIGHT?
MAKES SENSE!
SPEAKING OF WHICH, LATELY, EVEN WHEN I FIRE BIG SPELLS...
MY STAFF DOESN'T RECOIL AND HIT MY HEAD, SO MY CONTROL OVER MY MAGIC HAS STABILIZED!
I KNOW THAT FEELING.
IT'S NICE TO SEE YOUR EFFORT PAY OFF.

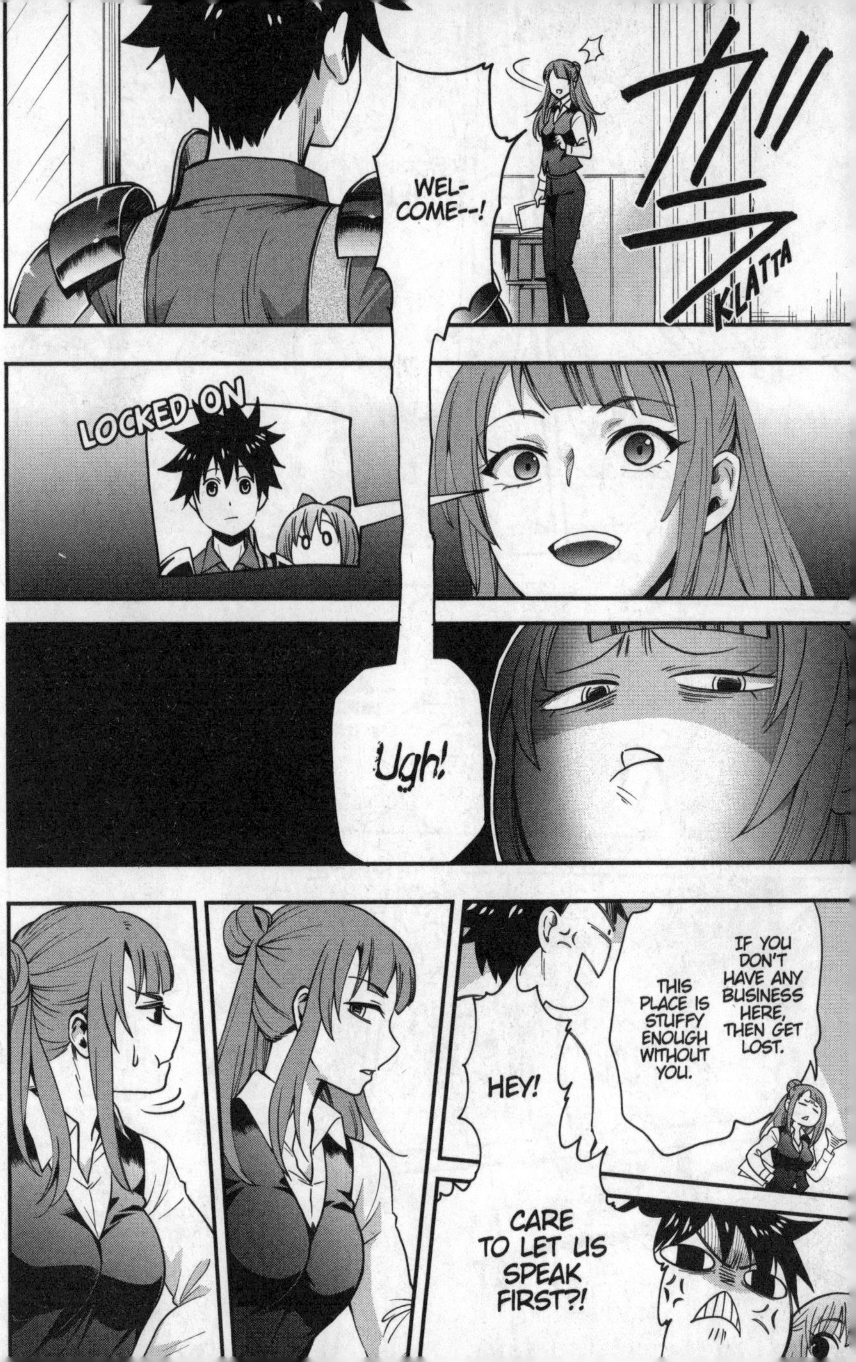
KLATTA
WEL-COME--!
LOCKED ON
Ugh!
IF YOU DON'T HAVE ANY BUSINESS HERE, THEN GET LOST.
THIS PLACE IS STUFFY ENOUGH WITHOUT YOU.
HEY!
CARE TO LET US SPEAK FIRST?!

I'VE BEEN...
WORRIED ABOUT YOU.
HAH?
-SNEER
YOU HAVEN'T STOPPED BY AT ALL LATELY...
so I thought you'd gone from invisible to nonexistent.
WOW, THANK YOU SO MUCH FOR YOUR CONCERN! IF ONLY I HAD A BETTER WAY TO EXPRESS MY GRATITUDE!

10 MINUTES LATER

MY STORE'S GONNA GET SHUT DOWN BY A FREAKING NOBODY!

AH HAA HA HAAA!!

DA-DOON

I'M GONNA GO OUT OF BUSINESS!

ROUGHLY FIVE THOUSAND.

HOW MANY DID YOU BRING?!

I'M SOBBING OVER HERE!

GLAD TO SEE YOU SO HAPPY!

HOW'D YOU EVEN GET THIS MANY?!

THIS IS A MONTH'S WORTH. I JUST WANTED TO SEE YOUR FACE WHEN WE TRIED SELLING IT ALL AT ONCE.

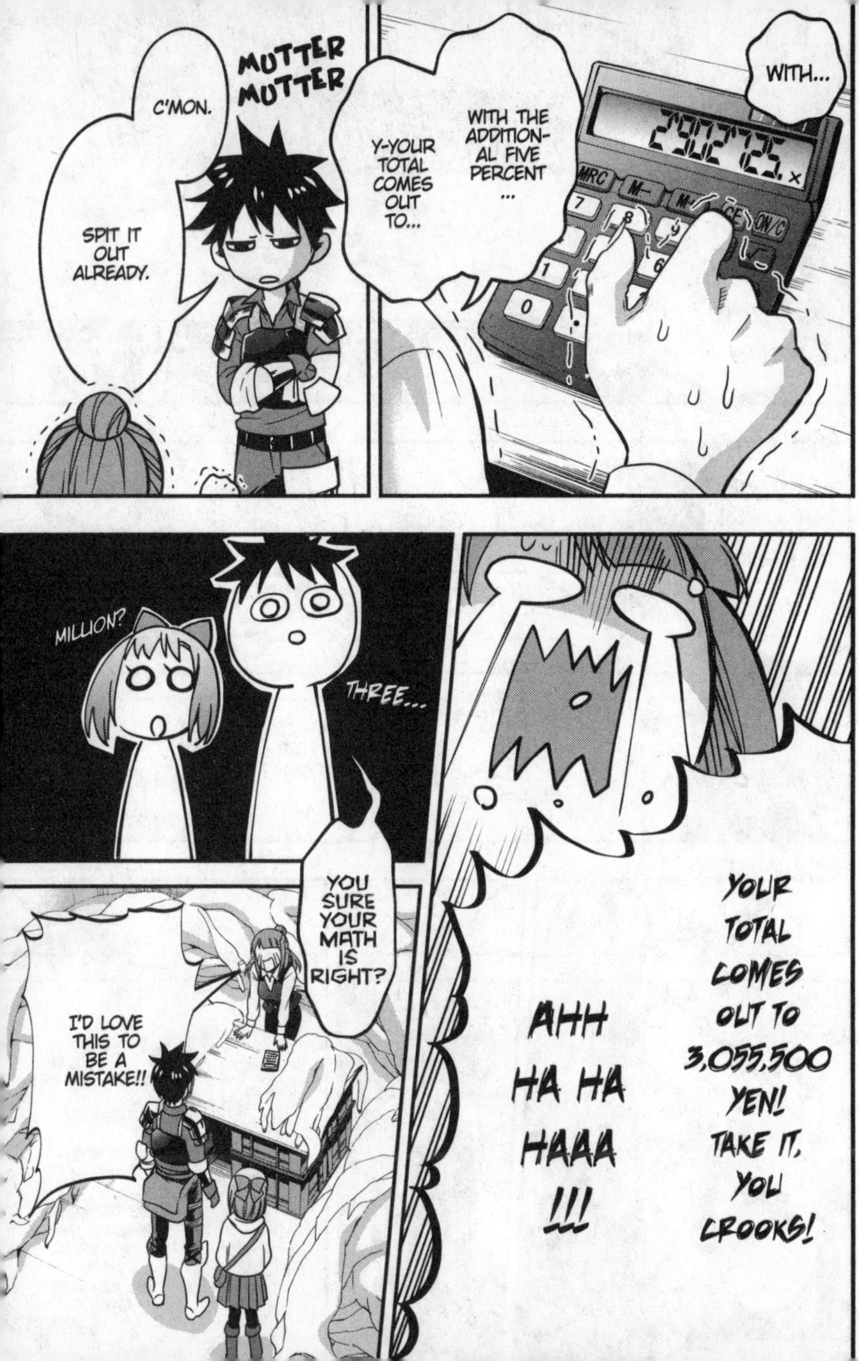
WITH...
2902725.
WITH THE ADDITIONAL FIVE PERCENT...
Y-YOUR TOTAL COMES OUT TO...
MUTTER MUTTER
C'MON.
SPIT IT OUT ALREADY.
YOUR TOTAL COMES OUT TO 3,055,500 YEN! TAKE IT, YOU CROOKS!
AHH HA HA HAAA!!!
THREE...
MILLION?
YOU SURE YOUR MATH IS RIGHT?
I'D LOVE THIS TO BE A MISTAKE!!

ALMOST FORGOT SOMETHING, AKANE.

MY SHOP IS GONNA GO BANKRUPT!

WAUGH!

WHAT DO YOU WANT?

WE NEED TO ORDER SOME ARMOR.

OUR IMMEDIATE GOAL IS THE MID-LEVELS.

BUT KAREN NEEDS A FULL-BODY SET.

MOST OF MY ARMOR IS ALREADY FROM THE MIDDLE-CLASS MODERN SERIES...

WHAT SPECIFICATIONS?

FWUP
GLINT

VERY WELL.

KRk KRk
FWP

UNFORTUNATELY, HERS GOT DESTROYED DURING THE INCIDENT WITH SHIKAMA'S PARTY.

I'M GOING TO GET BACK...
EVERY LAST YEN I JUST GAVE YOU.
BRING IT ON!!
JUST SO YOU KNOW, IF THE ARMOR SUCKS, WE'LL RETURN IT.
WHO DO YOU THINK YOU'RE TALKING TO?
BUCKLE DOWN, NOW.
H-HEY, MR. INVISIBLE.
HM?

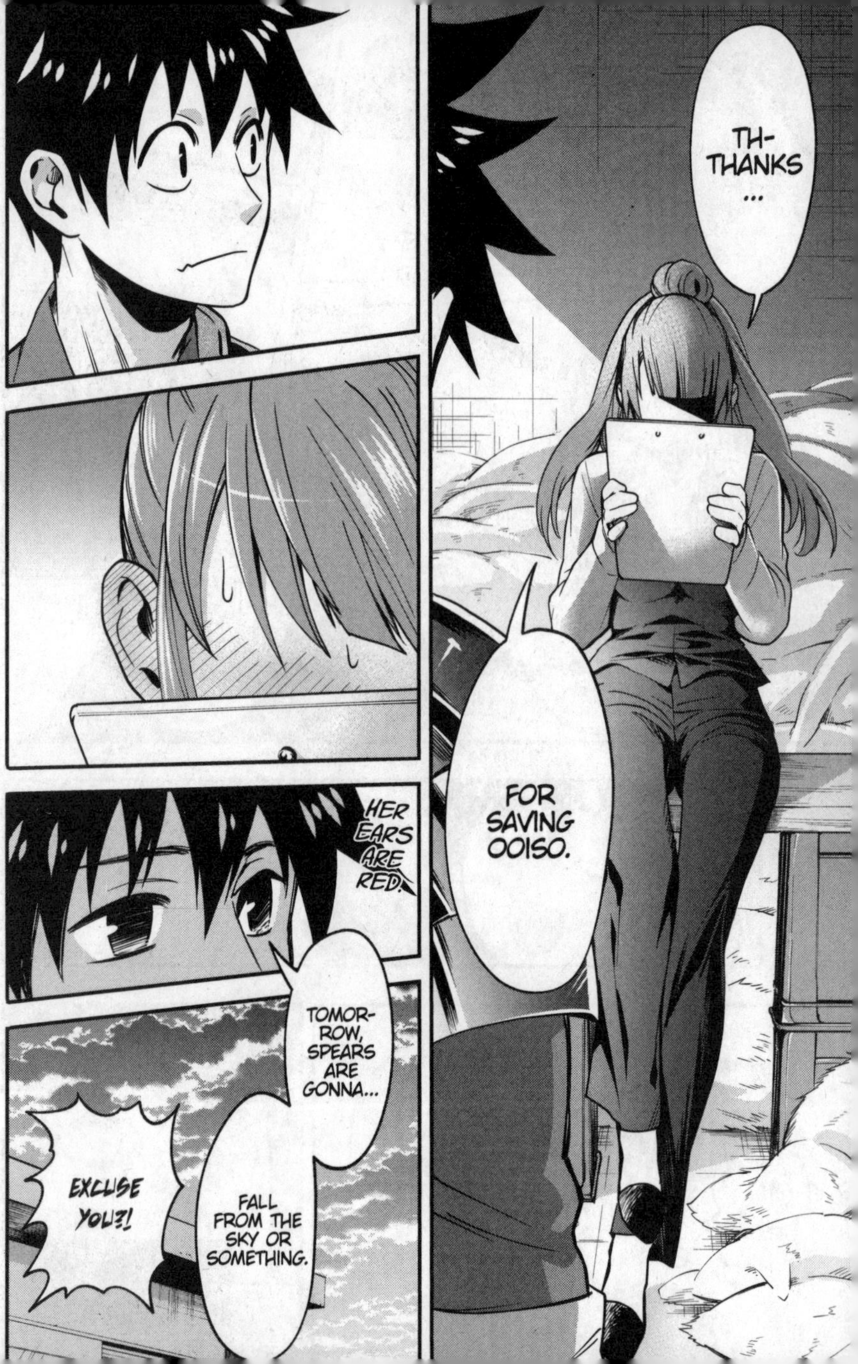
TH-THANKS ...
FOR SAVING OOISO.
HER EARS ARE RED.
TOMORROW, SPEARS ARE GONNA...
FALL FROM THE SKY OR SOMETHING.
EXCUSE YOU!?!

Level 6
POLYPHECOOOL!
VEGETABLES! BROTH! TEPPANYAKI!
FRIED TEMPURA! FRIED SANDWICHES!
Level 7
KROO!
MEAT...
Level 8

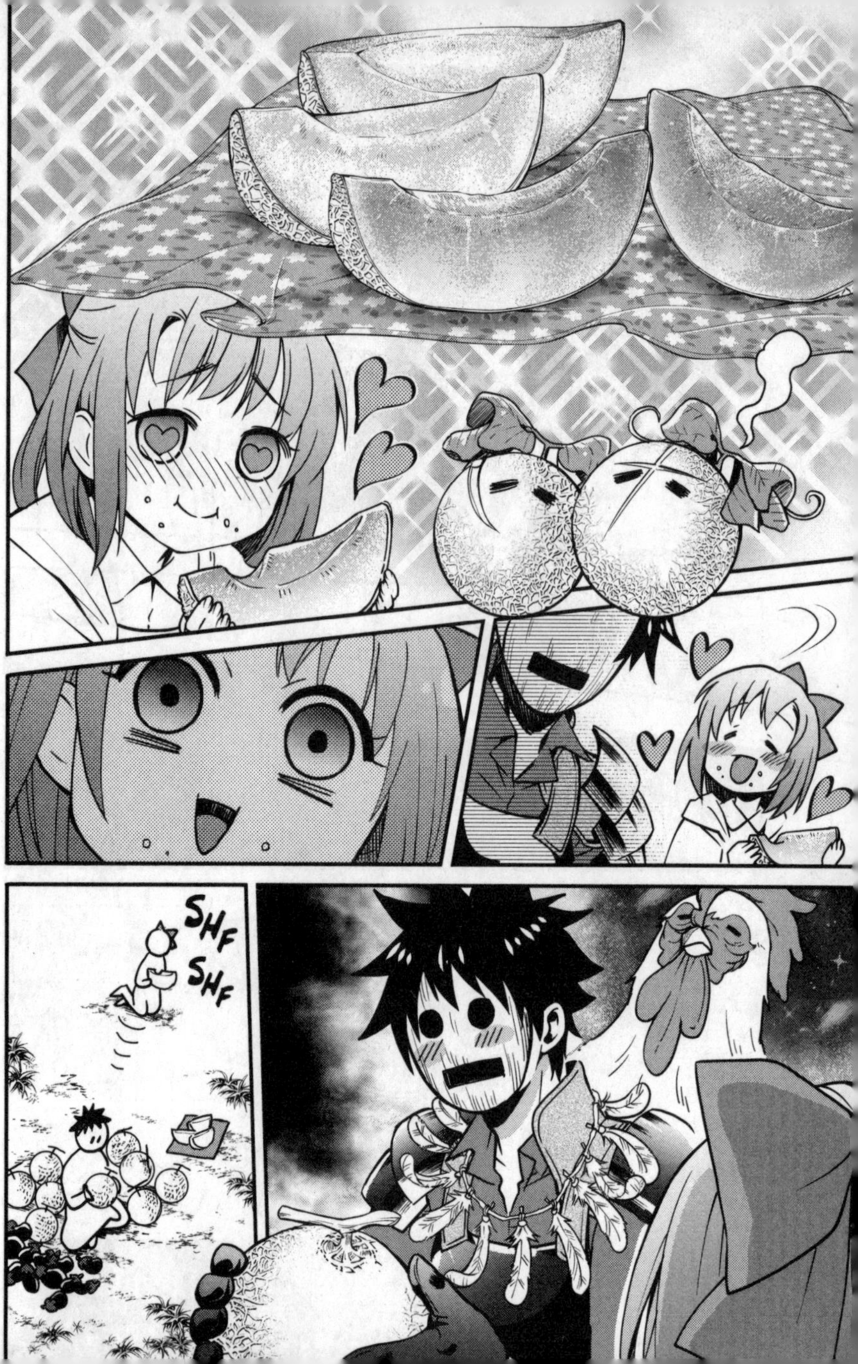
SHF
SHF

ANOTHER BIG BATCH? REALLY?

YEP! WHAT'S THE BOSS DROP?

THIS STONE IS A MAGIC TOOL.

IT HEATS UP WHEN YOU STRIKE IT. AT THIS SIZE, IT'S BEST SUITED FOR COOKING AND SUCH.

I SEE!

THIS IVY IS WORTH TEN THOUSAND YEN PER METER.

WHAT? IT IS?!

IT CAN BE TURNED INTO A STRONG BOWSTRING.

THIS IS A COCKS-COMB.

AND THIS NECKLACE...

I CAN'T BELIEVE YOU WORE IT.

MAKES SENSE.

HUH?

What if it's cursed?
DOESN'T LOOK CURSED TO ME.
YOUR CLOTHING STYLE IS CREEPY.
I'M TELLING YOU TO USE YOUR HEAD.
AS FOR WHAT IT DOES...
IT PROBABLY GIVES YOU A SMALL AGILITY BOOST.
WOW, THAT'S A KEEPER!
HEH HEH HEH HEH HEH HEH!
HERE WE GO!
Ichi
IT'S MY TIME TO SHINE !!
Purchase Order
Ichi
DUN
DN DN
DN DN
DN DN

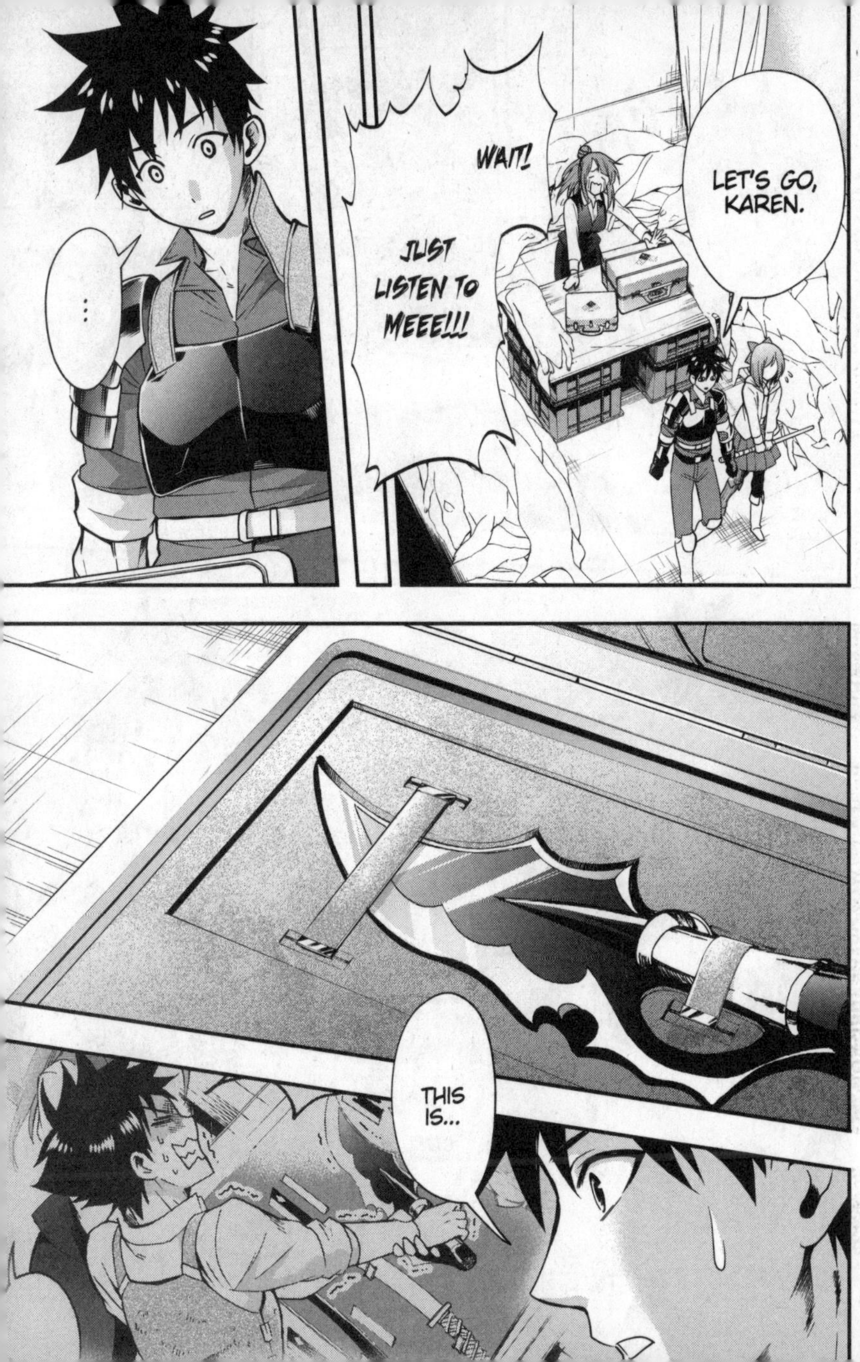
LET'S GO, KAREN.
WAIT!
JUST LISTEN TO MEEE!!!
...
THIS IS...

SHF
GRIP
A LITTLE HEAVY...
WHRR
LOOKS LIKE IT ACCEPTS YOU.
BUT IT FEELS GOOD IN MY HAND.
SHWP
THIS TIME.
DAMN HER!

HOW'S IT FEEL, KAREN?
GOOD!
OOOH!
IT'S A TAD RESTRICTIVE, BUT IT'LL WORK.
NOW I'VE GOT A FULL MODERN SERIES SET, TOO.
OUR THREE MILLION IS LONG GONE, THOUGH.

COULD YOU NOT?!! AND RAKE AKANE OVER THE COALS AGAIN! LET'S USE THIS NEW EQUIPMENT TO HUNT THE CRAP OUTTA SOME MONSTERS...

KAREN, WE'RE GOING TO THE DUNGEON.

LEVEL 8 TODAY?

WELL, WE'RE ABOUT TO ENTER THE MID-LEVELS... SO I WANNA EXPLORE LEVEL 9.

OKAY...

AWW... I WANNA EAT MORE MELON...

SLUMP.

Level 8

Level 9

I BET WE'LL FACE NEW MONSTERS.
LET'S KEEP OUR GUARD UP.
GOT IT!
!
RSTL
RSTL
KARABOSHI-SAN!
RSTL
RSTL
...
IT'S ...
SO CUTE!
DUN

SHLURR

HM?

ZRIK

ZRSH

THAT ASIDE... KAREN.

FELT LIKE CUTTING THROUGH PAPER.

THIS NEW WEAPON IS AWESOME!

I'M SORRY!

JUST BECAUSE IT'S CUTE DOESN'T MEAN IT'S NOT A MONSTER.

LET'S KEEP MOVING!

OKAY!

ONLY ONE ROOM LEFT.
MUST BE WHERE THE BOSS IS HIDING.
I'M GUESSING IT'LL BE A GIANT ANT-EATER!
NORMAL
BIG BOSS
YEAH, ME...
TOO.

IS IT A DEMI-HUMAN?!

A LONG-TONGUE!

IT'S EVEN WIELDING A WEAPON!

SURE LOOKS STRONG!

I'M SCARED...

FEAR MEANS SHE CAN SENSE THE DIFFERENCE IN STRENGTH.

BUT WE NEED TO OVERCOME THIS.

STAY HIDDEN AND ONLY ATTACK WHEN YOU'RE CERTAIN YOU'LL HIT IT.

WHAT SHOULD I DO?

KAREN, RHEA'S AMMO PROBABLY WON'T EVEN LEAVE A MARK.

I'LL CLOSE THE DISTANCE AND DEAL SOME DAMAGE.

UH...

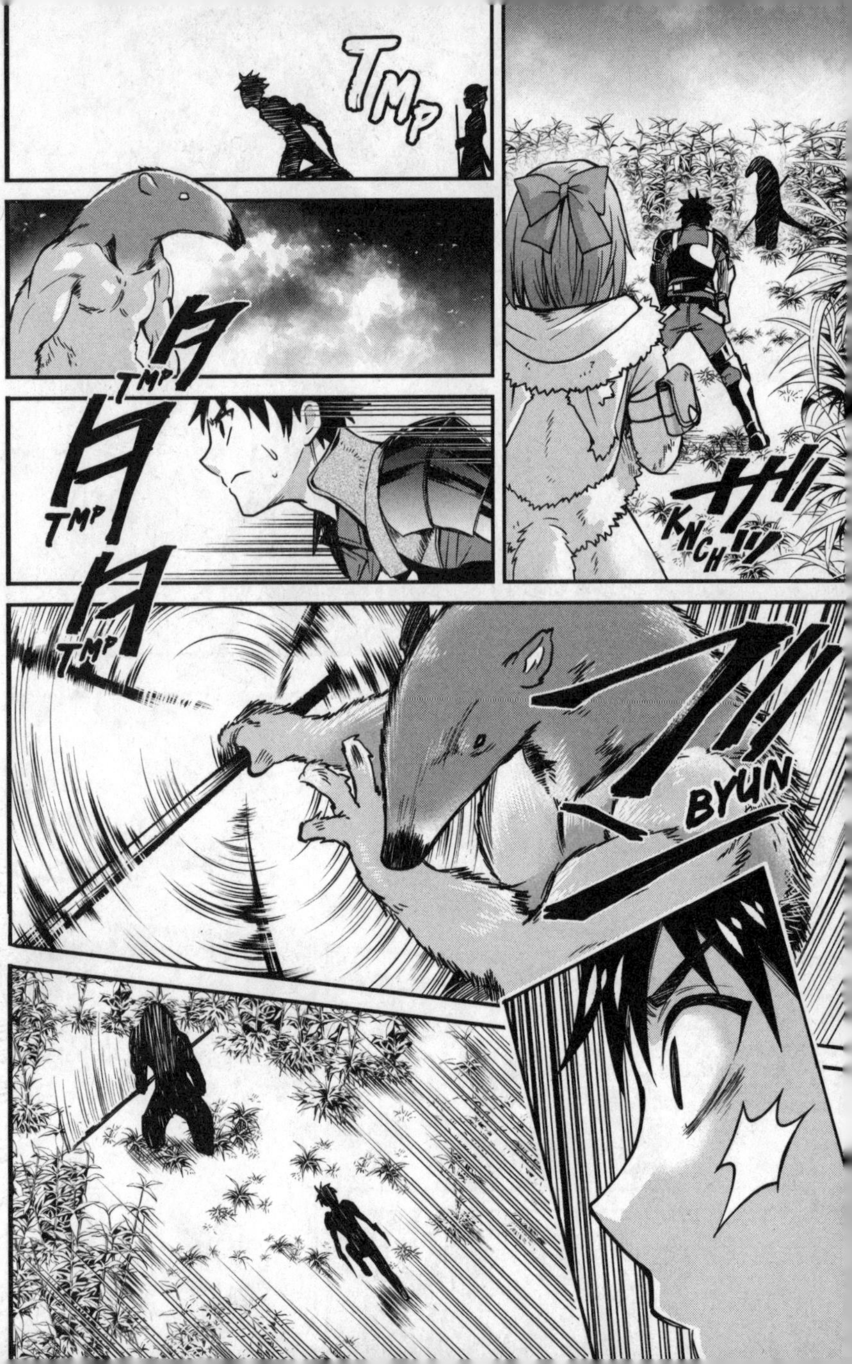
TMP
TMP
TMP
TMP
KNCH!!
BYUN

ZUOOOON
DAMN... THIS THING IS HUGE!
GLANG

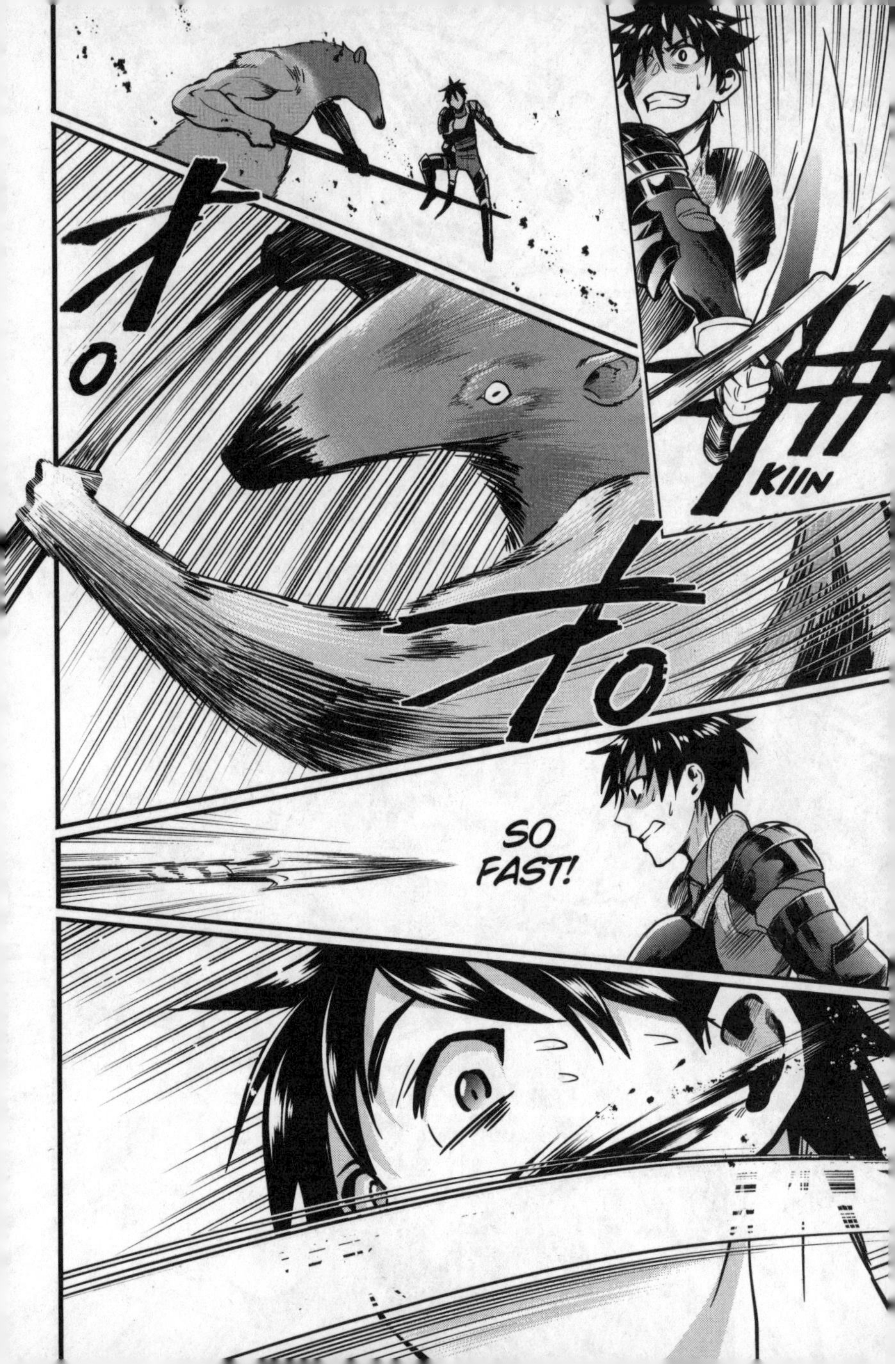
KIIN
SO FAST!

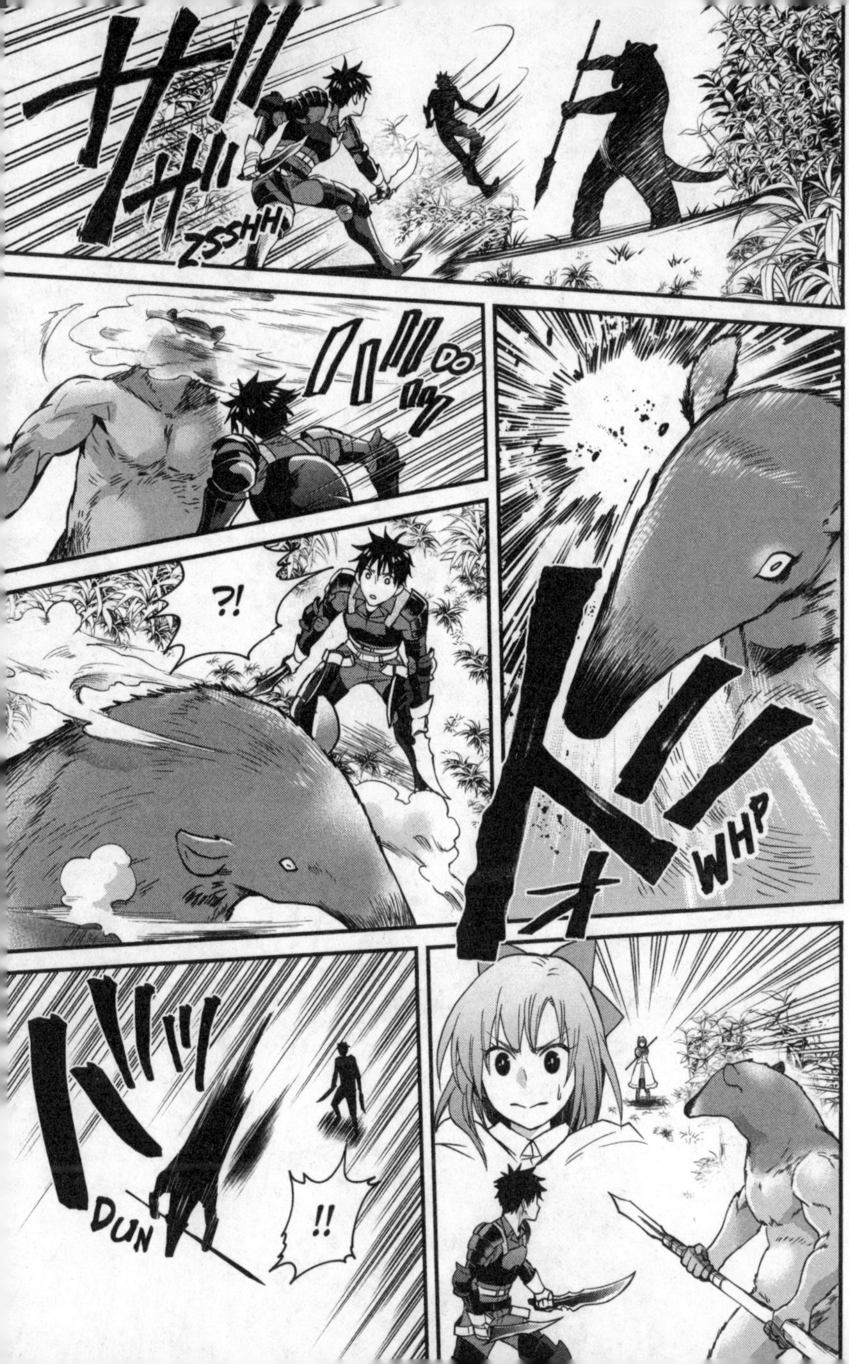
ZSSHH
DO
WHP
?!
DUN
!!

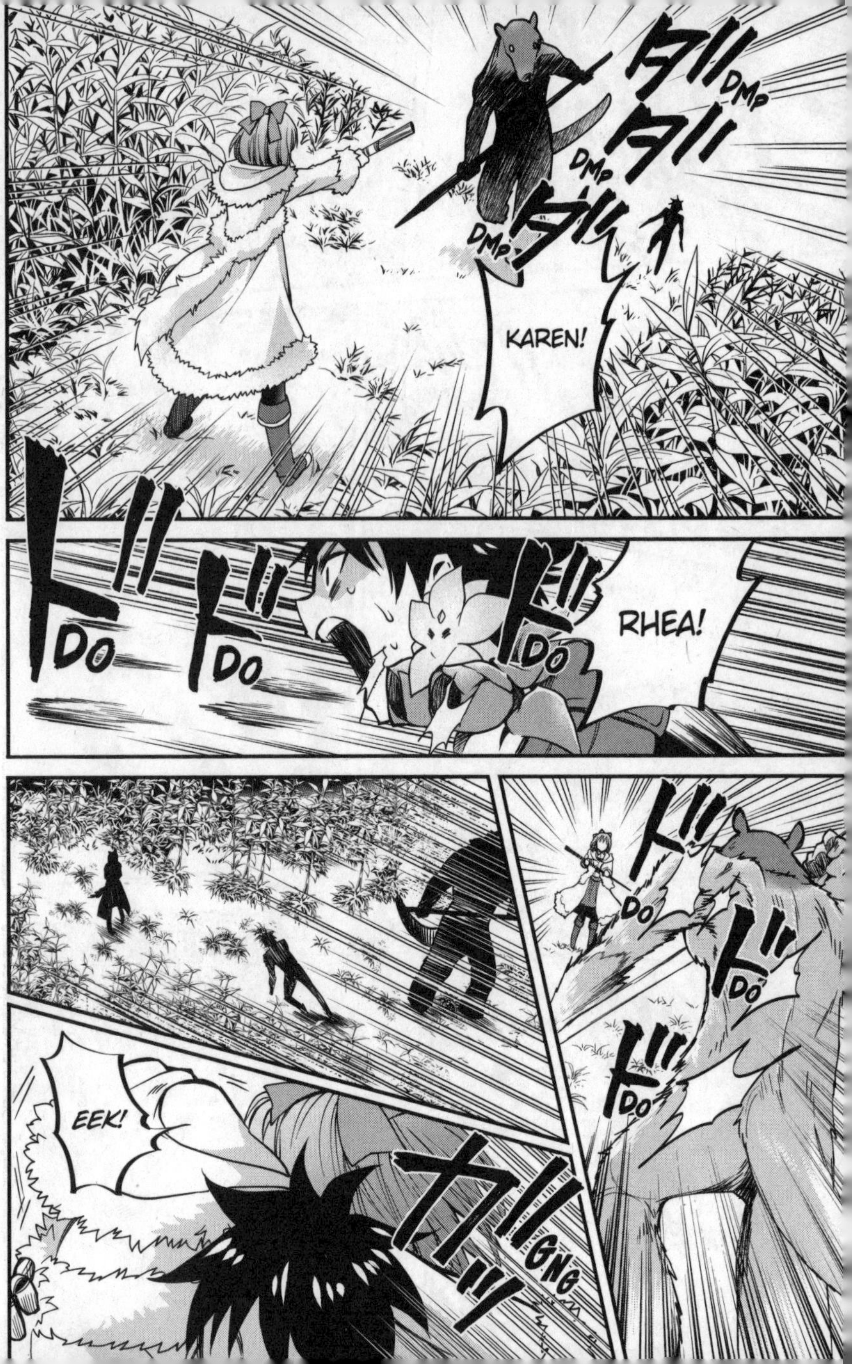

DMP
DMP
DMP
KAREN!
RHEA!
DO
DO
DO
DO
DO
DO
EEK!
GNG

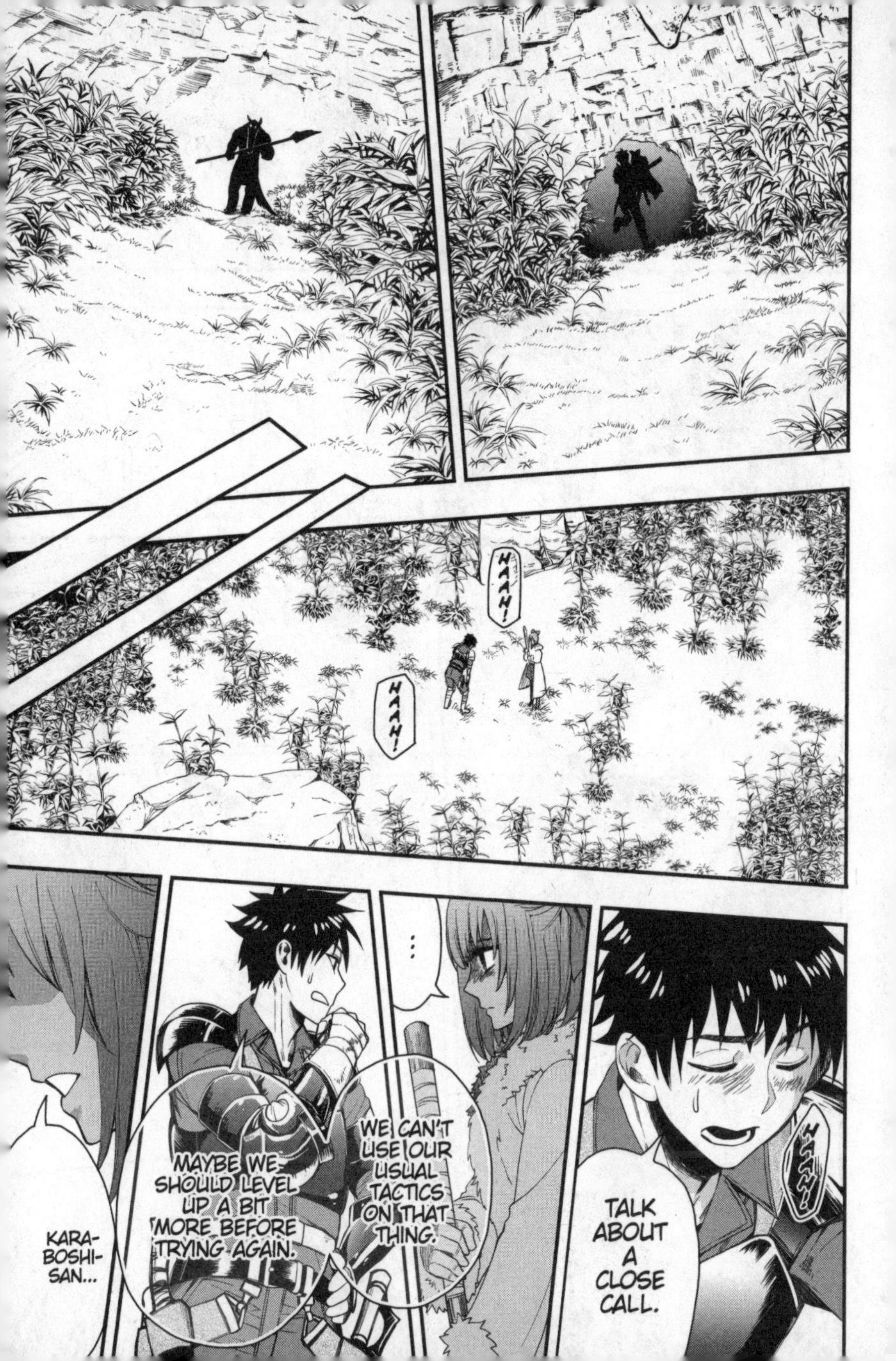
HAAAH!
HAAAH!
HAAAH!
TALK ABOUT A CLOSE CALL.
...
WE CAN'T USE OUR USUAL TACTICS ON THAT THING.
MAYBE WE SHOULD LEVEL UP A BIT MORE BEFORE TRYING AGAIN.
KARA-BOSHI-SAN...

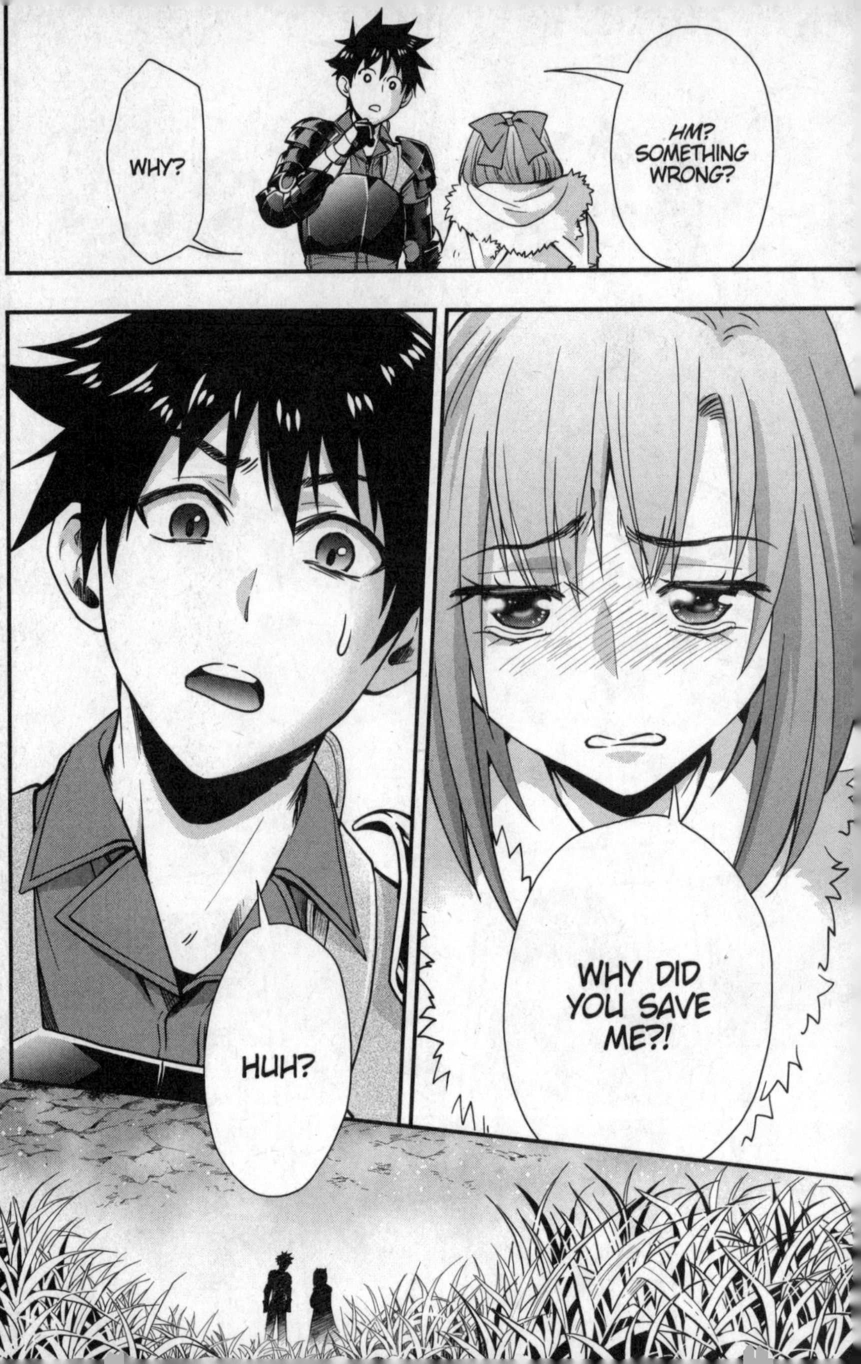
HM? SOMETHING WRONG?
WHY?
WHY DID YOU SAVE ME?!
HUH?

ザワ
MURMUR
ザワ
MURMUR
WHAT?
SERI-OUSLY?
ザワ
MURMUR
ISN'T THAT...
A RANKER'S PARTY? AERIAL?
THEY'RE IN SHAMBLES.
ザワ
MURMUR
ザワ
MURMUR
HAAAH~~~

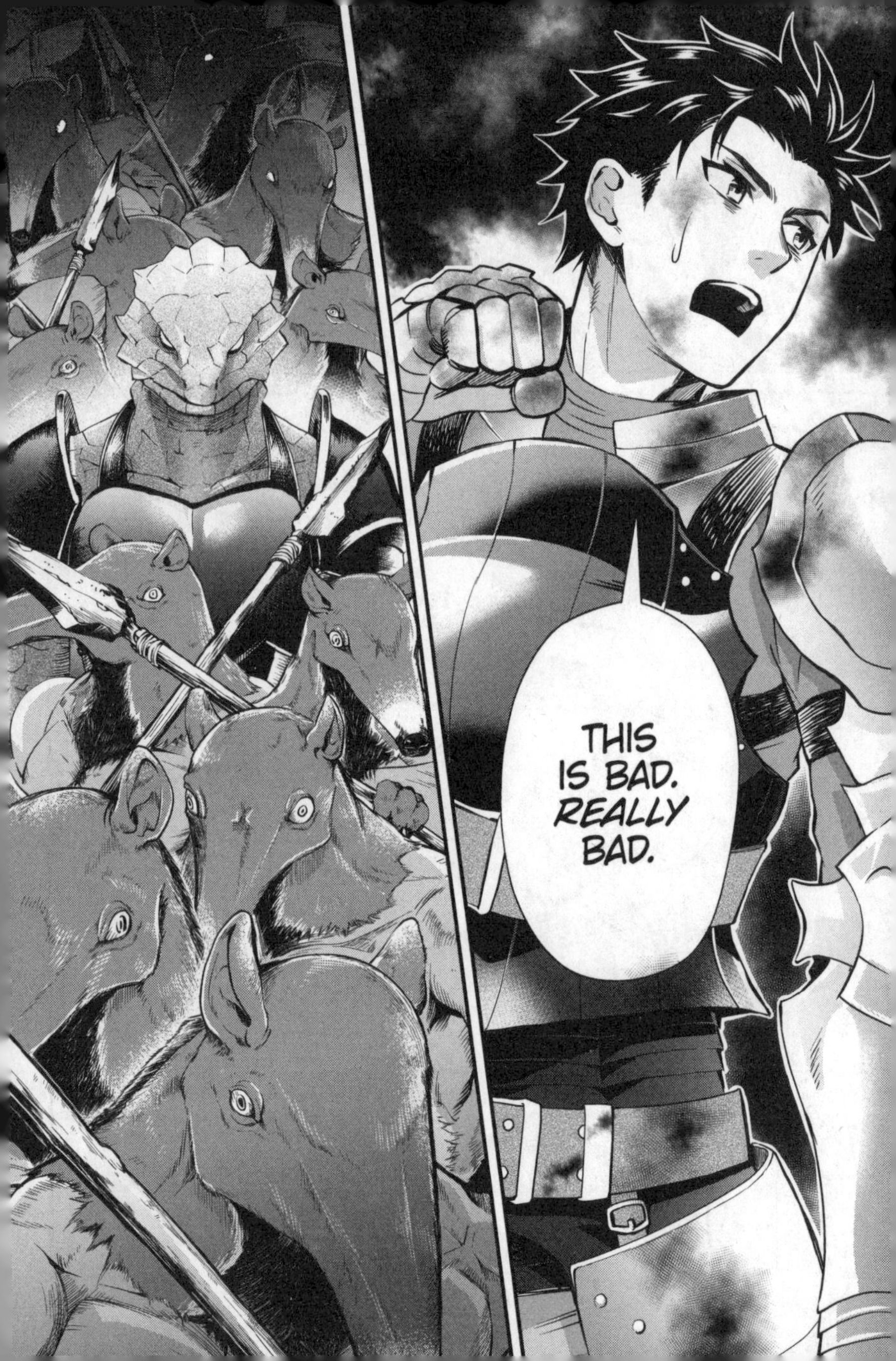
THIS IS BAD. *REALLY* BAD.

Chapter 19

WHAT DO YOU MEAN, WHY?

DO YOU THINK I CAN'T HANDLE MYSELF?

AM I THAT UNRELIABLE?

I ONLY SAVED YOU TO AVOID THE WORST-CASE SCEN--!

N-NO!

WE'RE A TEAM, AREN'T WE?!

WELL, YEAH.
THEN WHY DID YOU SAVE ME WHEN THE BEST-CASE SCENARIO WAS AT HAND?
THAT WAS THE BEST-CASE SCE-NARIO?
NOT THE WORST?
I KNOW I'M A WORRYWART WITH NO CONFIDENCE...
BUT I WANT TO BE A PROPER ADVEN-TURER, TOO.
I WANT TO DO ALL THIS ALONG-SIDE YOU.
SO PLEASE ...
JUST TRUST ME!!

WHAT DO YOU NEED ME TO DO?

?!

LET LOOSE!

BUT THAT'D PUT YOU IN DANG--!

DON'T WORRY ABOUT WHAT I'M DOING! INSTEAD, FIGHT WITH ALL YOUR MIGHT!

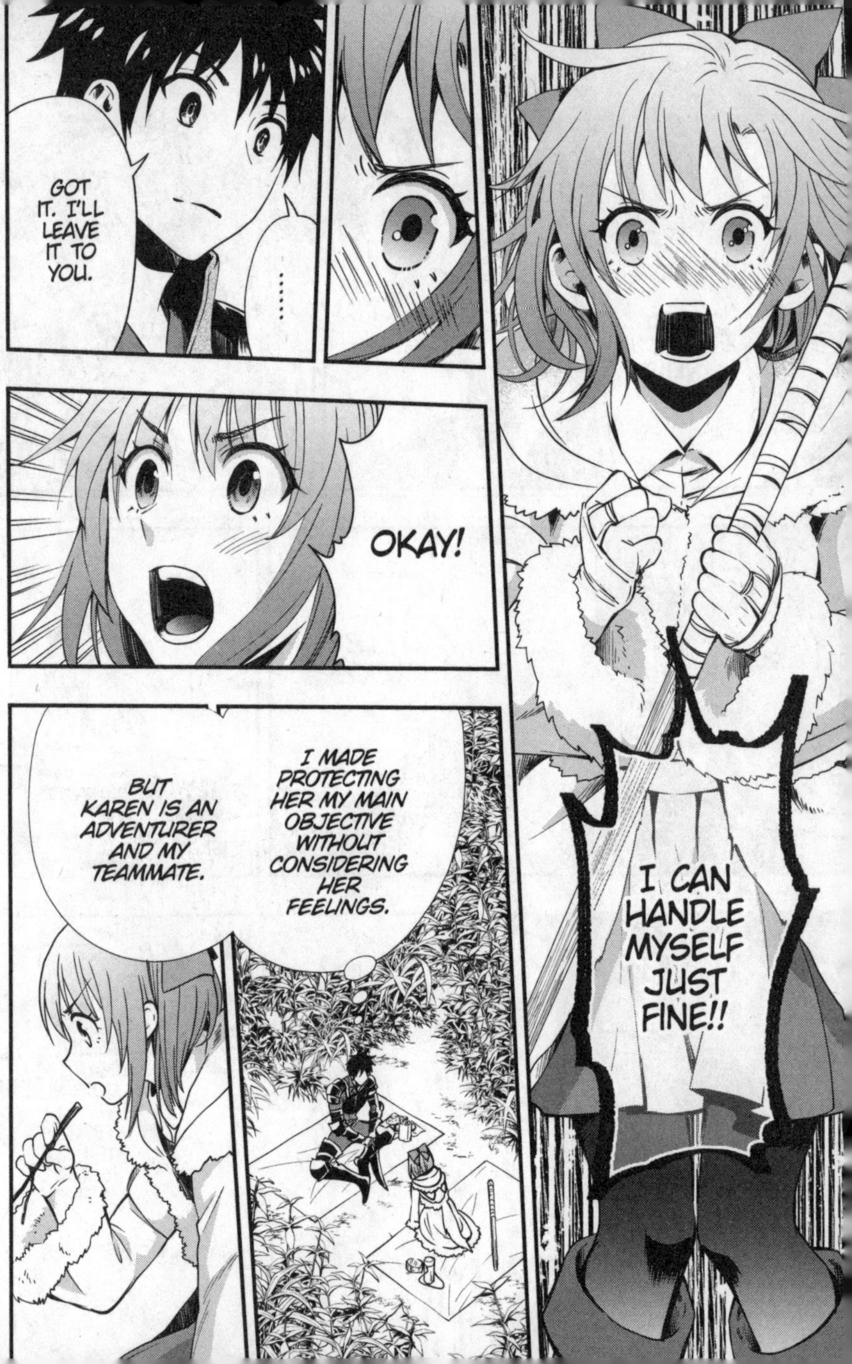
I CAN HANDLE MYSELF JUST FINE!!
GOT IT. I'LL LEAVE IT TO YOU.
......
OKAY!
I MADE PROTECTING HER MY MAIN OBJECTIVE WITHOUT CONSIDERING HER FEELINGS.
BUT KAREN IS AN ADVENTURER AND MY TEAMMATE.

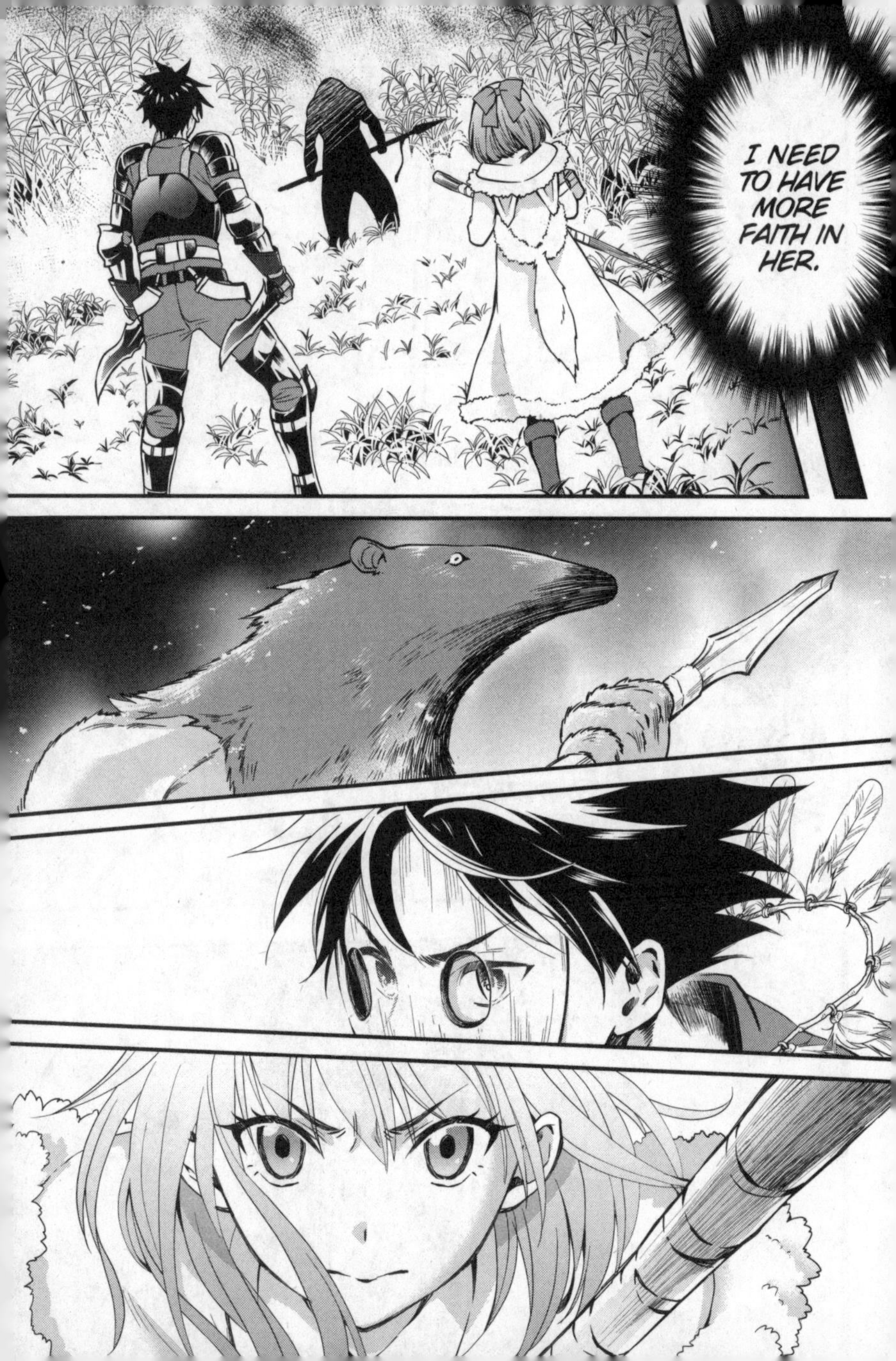
I NEED TO HAVE MORE FAITH IN HER.

DOON

LIFT

THAT'S IT!!

GLARE

FWP FWP

SHWF

?!

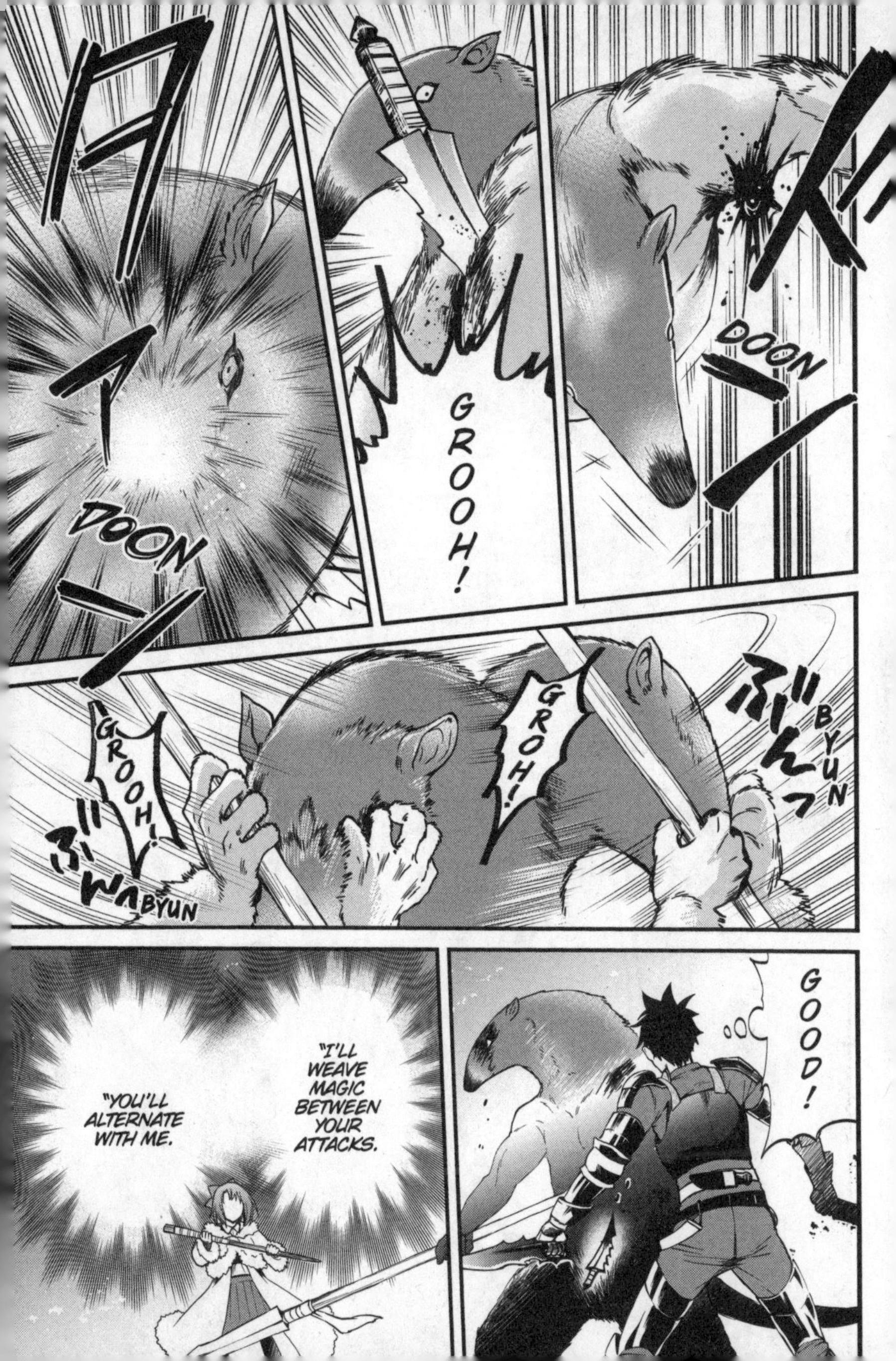
DOON
GROOOH!
DOON
BYUN
GROH!
GROOOH!
BYUN
GOOOD!
"I'LL WEAVE MAGIC BETWEEN YOUR ATTACKS.
"YOU'LL ALTERNATE WITH ME.

"THE FIRST FIGHT MADE ME REALIZE THAT LONG-TONGUES HAVE FORESIGHT.
"WE'LL USE THAT AGAINST IT!!"
SWAY
DWUMP

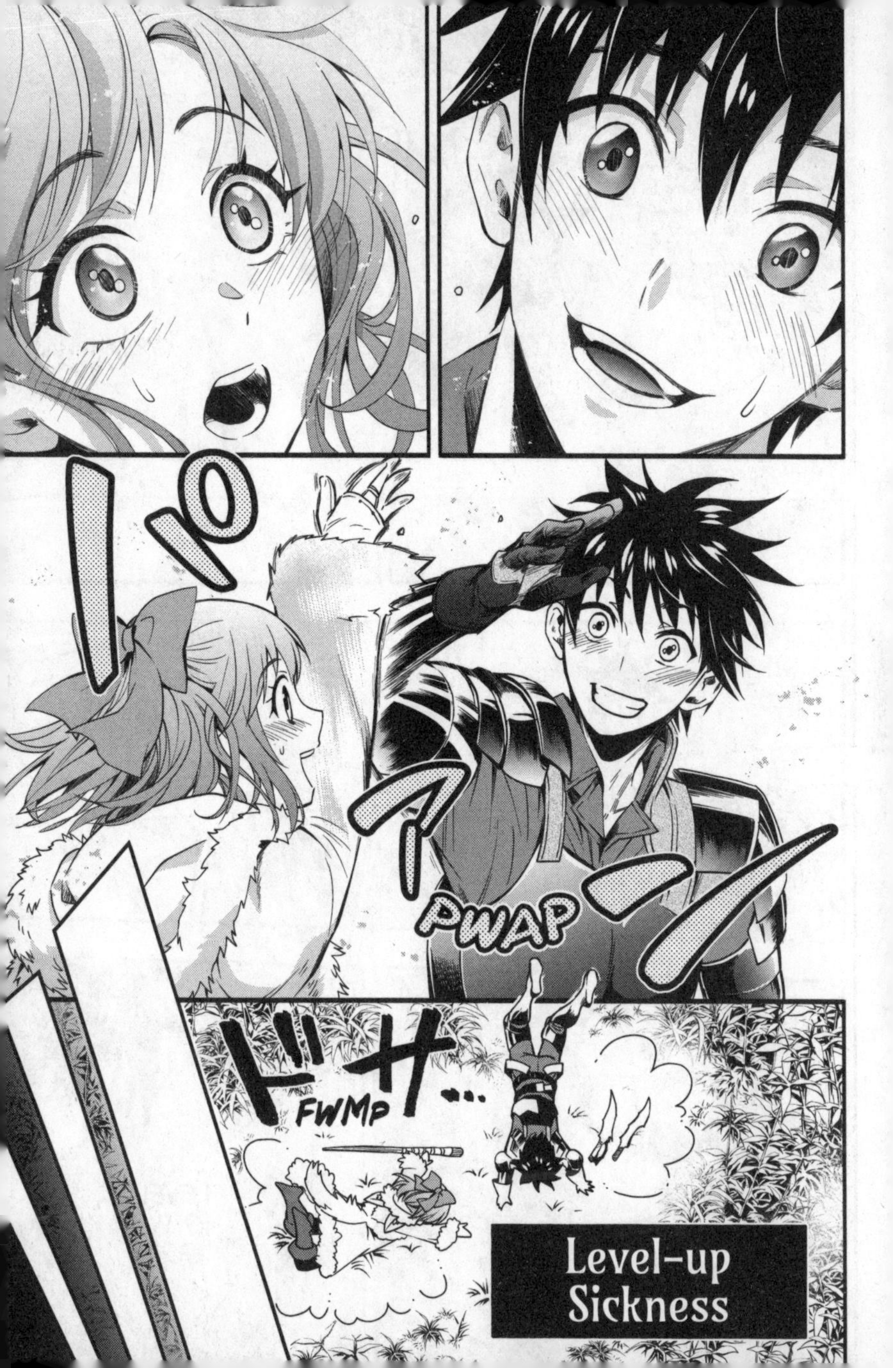
PWAP
FWMP
Level-up Sickness

IT DROPPED A WHOLE BUNCH OF DIFFERENT SPEARS.
WE DON'T SPECIALIZE IN THESE, SO WE CAN'T EQUIP THEM.
WHAT ABOUT THESE SMALL ONES?
SHWF
HUH?
SHWF
DOOOOOM
GUESS YOU CAN'T EQUIP THIS, EITHER.
BAD RHEA!
WAIT, WHAT? SEEMS I CAN. MIND IF I TAKE IT?
SLUMP
GO FOR IT!
SULK
IT'S TIME!
TO LEVEL 10 WE GO!!

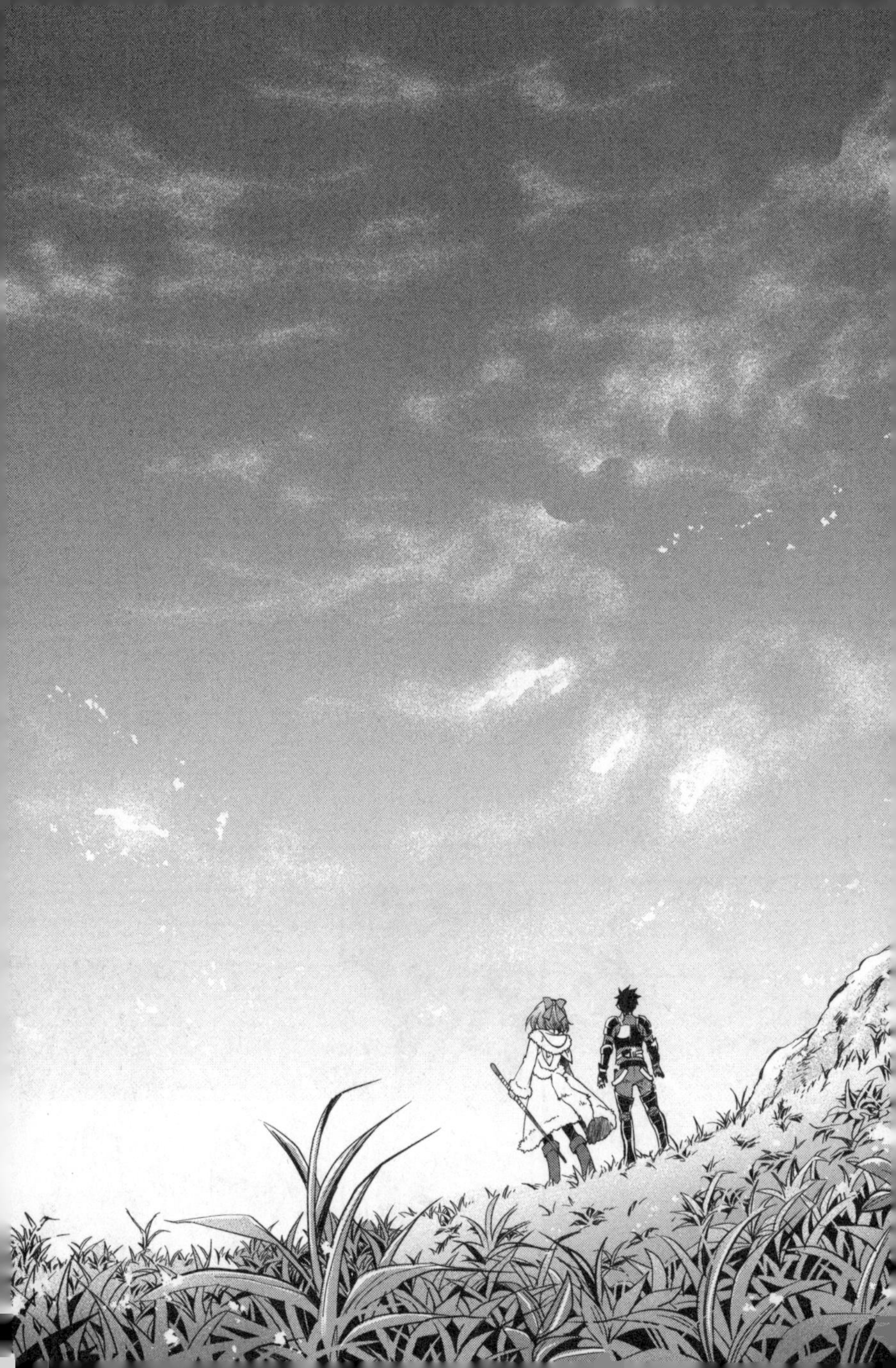

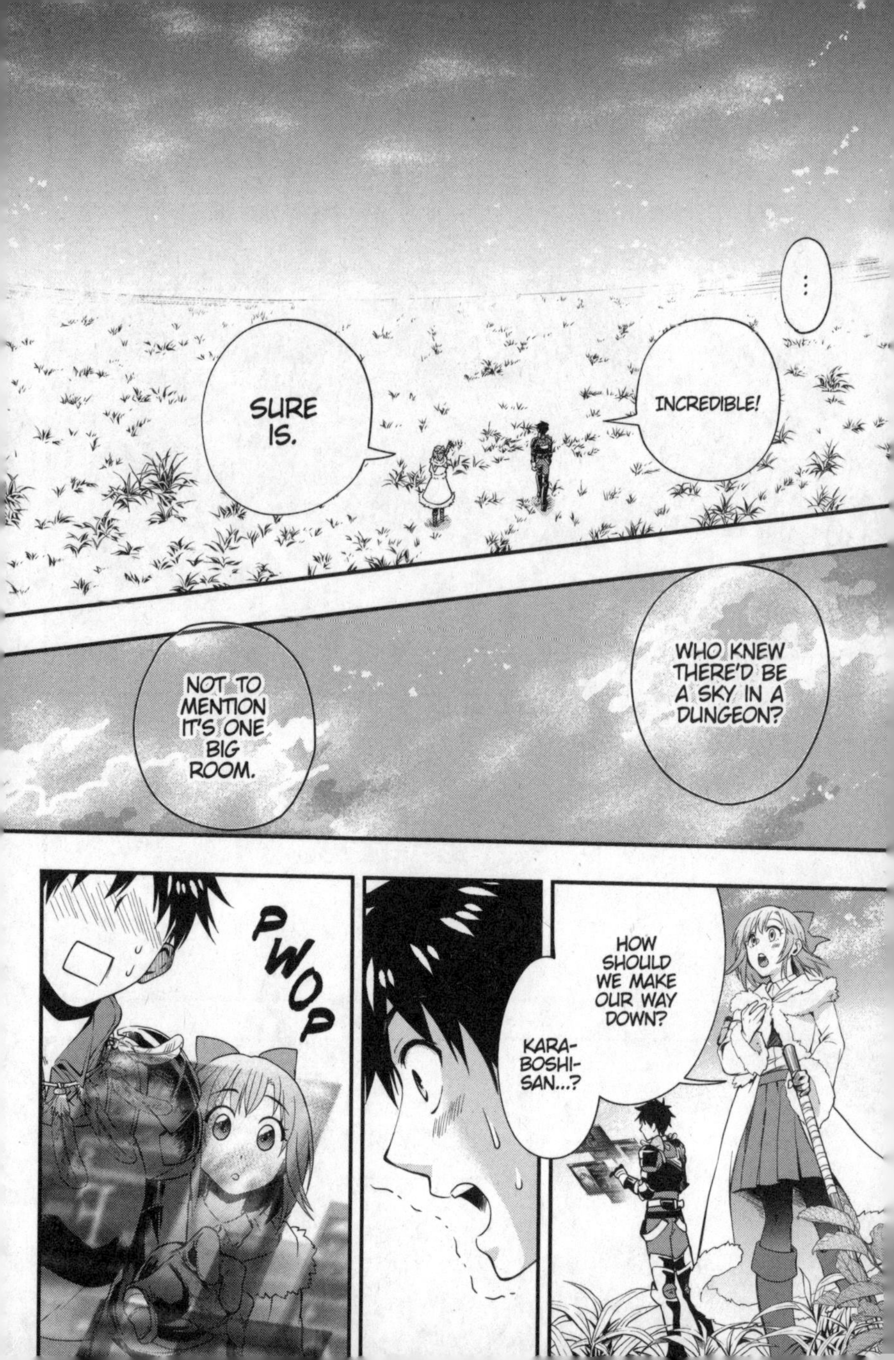
…
INCREDIBLE!
SURE IS.
WHO KNEW THERE'D BE A SKY IN A DUNGEON?
NOT TO MENTION IT'S ONE BIG ROOM.
HOW SHOULD WE MAKE OUR WAY DOWN?
KARA-BOSHI-SAN…?
PWOP

I UNLOCKED DIVINE PROTECTION!

AGE: 27 GENDER: MALE
SKILL POINTS
5
RANK: F
DIVINE PROTECTION: THAT OF CLOAKS <????>

GROWTH ACCELERATION — MAX/5
TAMING — 1/5
NEW DIVINE PROTECTION — 1/3

WH-WHAT KIND OF SKILL IS THAT?

SUPPOSEDLY, IT'S A BLESSING FROM A GOD!

MASATSUGU-SAN HAS IT, TOO! DELVING DOWN TO THE MID-LEVELS SEEMS TO BE THE KEY!

TH-THAT'S AMAZING!!

YEAH! BUT...

WHAT DOES "THAT OF CLOAKS" MEAN?

IS THERE...A GOD OF CLOAKS?

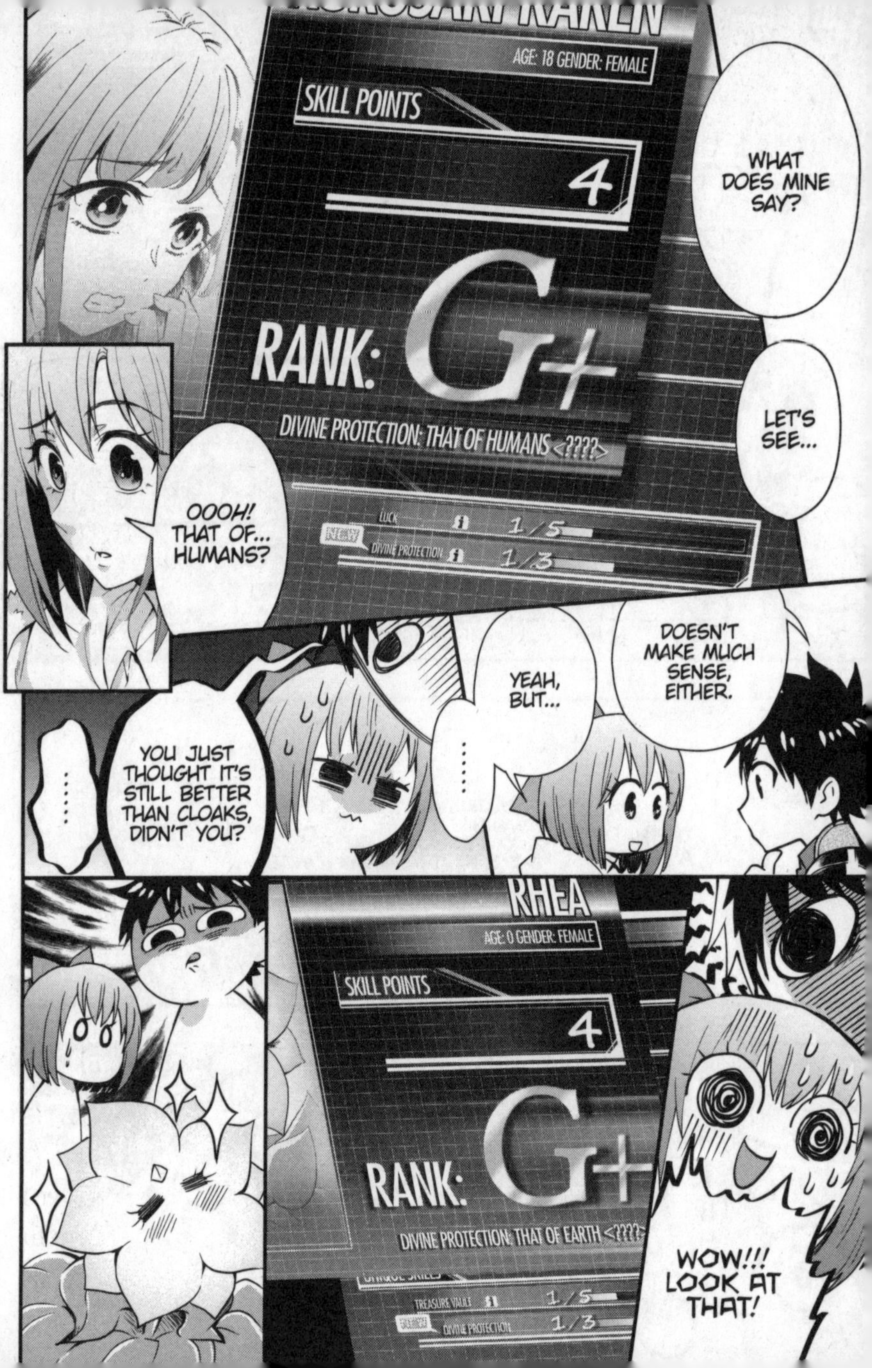
AGE: 18 GENDER: FEMALE
SKILL POINTS
4
RANK: G+
DIVINE PROTECTION: THAT OF HUMANS <????>
LUCK 1/5
NEW
DIVINE PROTECTION 1/3
WHAT DOES MINE SAY?
LET'S SEE...
OOOH! THAT OF... HUMANS?
DOESN'T MAKE MUCH SENSE, EITHER.
YEAH, BUT...
......
YOU JUST THOUGHT IT'S STILL BETTER THAN CLOAKS, DIDN'T YOU?
......
WOW!!! LOOK AT THAT!
RHEA
AGE: 0 GENDER: FEMALE
SKILL POINTS
4
RANK: G+
DIVINE PROTECTION: THAT OF EARTH <????>
TREASURE VAULT 1/5
DIVINE PROTECTION 1/3

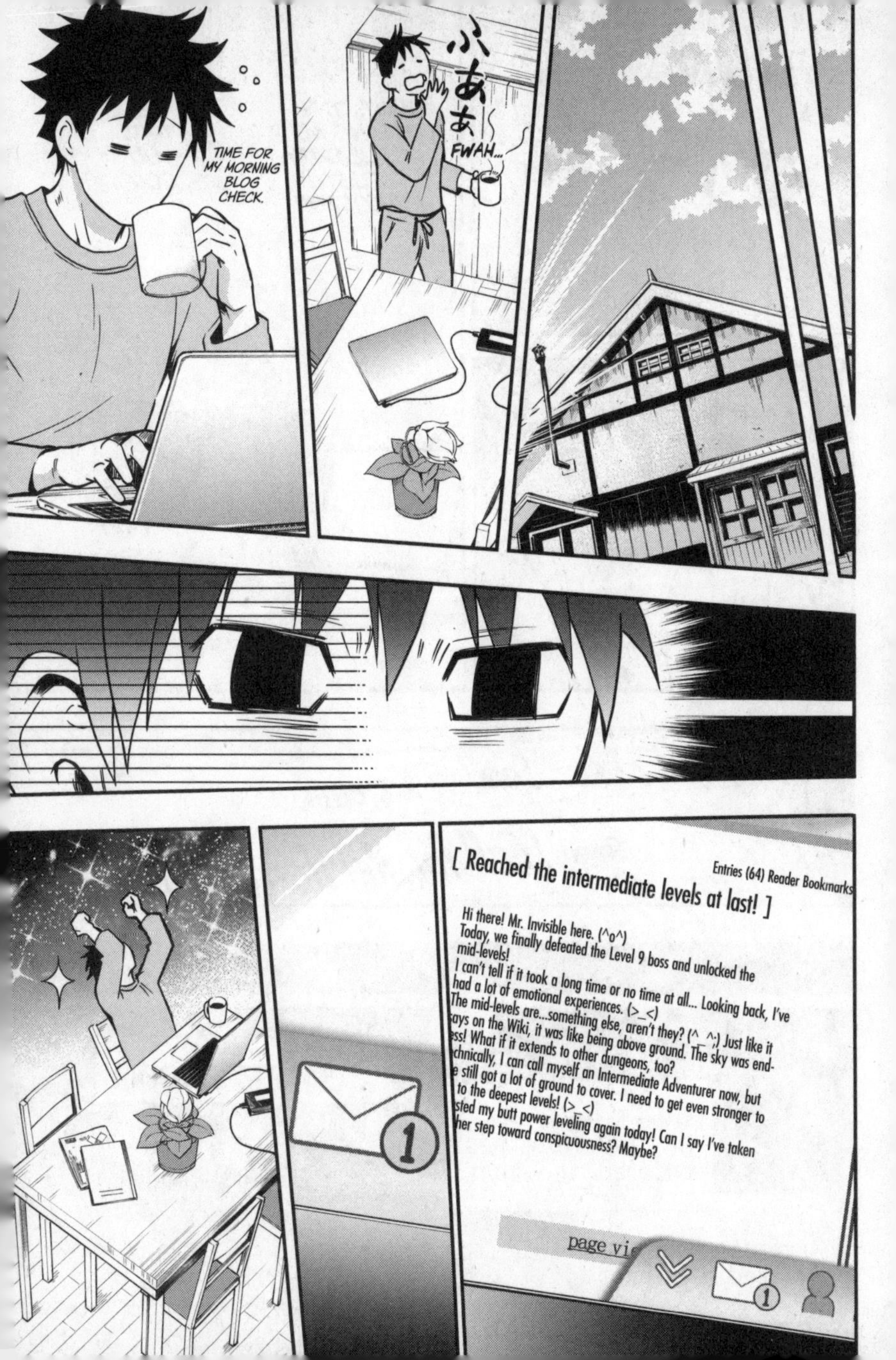
ふあぁ
FWAH...
TIME FOR MY MORNING BLOG CHECK.
[Reached the intermediate levels at last!]
Entries (64) Reader Bookmarks
Hi there! Mr. Invisible here. (^o^)
Today, we finally defeated the Level 9 boss and unlocked the
mid-levels!
I can't tell if it took a long time or no time at all... Looking back, I've
had a lot of emotional experiences. (>_<)
The mid-levels are...something else, aren't they? (^_^;) Just like it
says on the Wiki, it was like being above ground. The sky was end-
ess! What if it extends to other dungeons, too?
chnically, I can call myself an Intermediate Adventurer now, but
e still got a lot of ground to cover. I need to get even stronger to
to the deepest levels! (>_<)
sted my butt power leveling again today! Can I say I've taken
her step toward conspicuousness? Maybe?
page vi
1
1

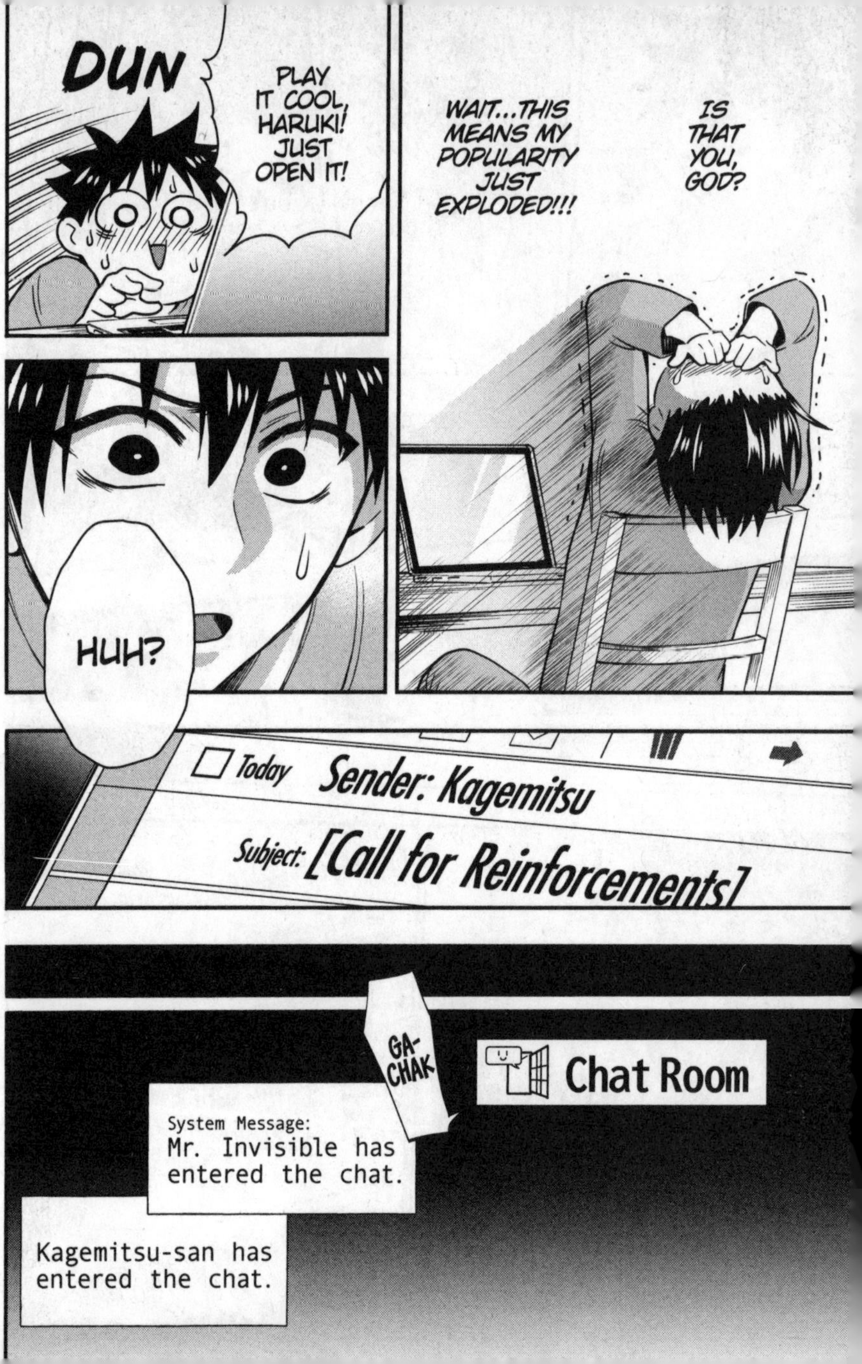
WAIT...THIS MEANS MY POPULARITY JUST EXPLODED!!!
IS THAT YOU, GOD?
DUN
PLAY IT COOL, HARUKI! JUST OPEN IT!
HUH?
Today
Sender: Kagemitsu
Subject: [Call for Reinforcements]
Chat Room
GA-CHAK
System Message:
Mr. Invisible has entered the chat.
Kagemitsu-san has entered the chat.

Sorry about the sudden message.
It's cool, I was just surprised.
Hard to believe Hokkaido's top Ranker, Kagemitsu-san, would contact me.
C'mon, man... I'm not that famous.
Hahaha! I'll take that as a compliment.
So, what's up?
Why do you need reinforce-ments?
No, really! I might be stuck in the middle of nowhere, but these days...
when people think Hokkaido, they think bears, crabs, and Kagemitsu!!
KAGEMITSU

You hear about the monster swarm in one of Chikaho's mid-levels?
News to me! Which level?
BF9
BF10
Level 10. I want you to help take it down.
Why me?
Heard a rumor that you exterminated one. Plus, you reached the mid-levels, which makes you an Intermediate Adventurer.
I only just did that. I'm not strong enough for this.
Won't know until you try. At this rate, the monsters will overrun us and cause a Stampede.

Sorry. I'm really not strong enough. I haven't even fought Level 10 monsters yet.
Oh. That sucks.
I figured even participating in the attack plan would make you **stand out** and
I'LL DO IT! LET ME IN!!!
Wow, okay.
カタ KLAKA
カタ KLAKA
カタ KLAKA
カタ KLAKA

THIS IS THE HOME OF HOKKAIDO'S TOP RANKER, HUH?!
BI
BA-DMP BA-DMP
GA-CHAK
HELLO...
THERE?!
GREETINGS. I'M MR. INVISIBLE.
JOLT

OH, HEY.
YOU'RE HERE.
!
HELLO, I'M MR. INVISIBLE.
KAGEMITSU. GREAT TO MEET YOU.
OH MAN!
HE SPARKLES! WILD!
FEELS LIKE HE'S ERASING MY PRESENCE, THOUGH.
BEEEEAM

NICE TO MEET YOU!	HEY...
	UH, HI.
	G-GLAD TO BE WORKING WITH YOU.

LET ME INTRODUCE YOU TO THE OTHER MEMBERS OF AERIAL.

STARTING FROM THE RIGHT, THIS IS YOSHI. HE USES A BOW.

BECKY HERE ALSO USES A BOW.

VAN USES A LONGSWORD, LIKE ME.

AND FINALLY, DORANEKO USES A SPEAR!

JOLT

I'M MR. INVISIBLE. I'M HAPPY TO WORK WITH YOU, TOO.

BOW

I HEARD THE RUMORS, BUT SEEING IT UP CLOSE IS HELLA SCARY.

WHAT?!

NOT AT ALL!

DO THEY ALL HAVE SOCIAL ANXIETY?

ISN'T YOUR MASK THE PROBLEM?!

I GUESS YOU'VE GOT A POINT.
SHOCK
YOUR PHYSICAL PRESENCE IS SO WEAK IT LOOKS LIKE THE MASK IS FLOATING.
THAT'S AN AMAZING SKILL YOU'VE GOT THERE.
HUH?
......
IT'S NATURAL.
WHAT?
FWP
HE DISAPPEARED?!
MY PRESENCE IS NATURALLY WEAK!
I FEEL YOU, MR. INVISIBLE!!
GRIP
I'VE ALWAYS WANTED TO BE A NINJA!!!
SORRY?
WHAT?

KAGE-MI-TSU-SAN.
LET'S PLAY SOCCER!
HE'S SO BAD AT THIS!
HEY!
FOUND HIM!
WHAT'RE YOU DOING?
I WANT IT SO BAD, BUT MY PRESENCE HAS ALWAYS BEEN TOO STRONG!
HE'S AT IT AGAIN!!
I WANT WHAT YOU HAVE!!
I WANT WHAT YOU HAVE!
EXCUSE ME!
ISN'T IT ABOUT TIME WE START THIS MEETING?!
I'LL GO MAKE SOME TEA.
LET ME HELP.
YES, MA'AM.
LIKE I SAID, I WANT YOU TO HELP US FEND OFF A MONSTER SWARM.
WHAT MONSTERS ARE IN THE SWARM?

MOSTLY LONG-TONGUES.
THE BOSS IS A REAL PAIN IN THE ASS.
I DEFEATED ONE RECENTLY, SO THAT'S FINE.
BUT YOU OPERATE ON LEVEL 24. WHAT DO YOU NEED ME FOR?
NOT ONLY IS THE LIZARDMAN A HIGH-LEVEL DEMI-HUMAN, IT'S A RARE SPECIES.
ONE THAT NORMALLY APPEARS ON LEVEL 30.

SHIVER
LEVEL 30?!
CLENCH
HEARING THAT JUST MAKES ME LESS CONFIDENT.
SERIOUSLY. WHY ARE YOU ASKING ME, SPECIFICALLY?
BE-CAUSE...
ONLY YOU'RE FIT FOR THE JOB.
?
OKAY, BUT WHY?!
CAN YOU THINK OF ANY OTHER IDIOT...
WHO WOULD CUT INTO THE HEART OF A MONSTER SWARM JUST FOR THE STREET CRED?

DAZE

THERE'S ANOTHER REASON, TOO.

MOST OF THE STRONG ADVENTURERS ARE ON THEIR WAY TO SHINJUKU.

THE ADVENTURERS THAT REMAIN ARE CASUAL NOVICES.

THERE'D BE A LOT OF CASUALTIES IF WE ASKED THEM TO HELP.

BETTER TO GO WITH A SMALL NUMBER OF SKILLED FIGHTERS, RIGHT?

I SEE.

"IF THINGS GET BAD, WE'LL WITHDRAW."

"BESIDES, WE'RE NOT TRYING TO PULL THIS OFF IN ONE GO."

"WE CAN PICK THEM OFF ACROSS SEVERAL ASSAULTS."

"WE'LL BACK YOU UP WITH EVERYTHING WE'VE GOT."

"I DON'T HAVE MUCH EXPERIENCE WITH THINGS THIS BIG."

"I'M NOT SURE HOW WELL I'D DO."

"I GET TO FIGHT ALONGSIDE RANKERS!"

GRIP
LET'S DO THIS!
DUN
I HEAR YOU LOUD AND CLEAR!
WHAT DO YOU NEED ME TO DO?!
OOOOH!
YOU'RE IN?!
GREAT!
IN THAT CASE, WE NEED YOU...

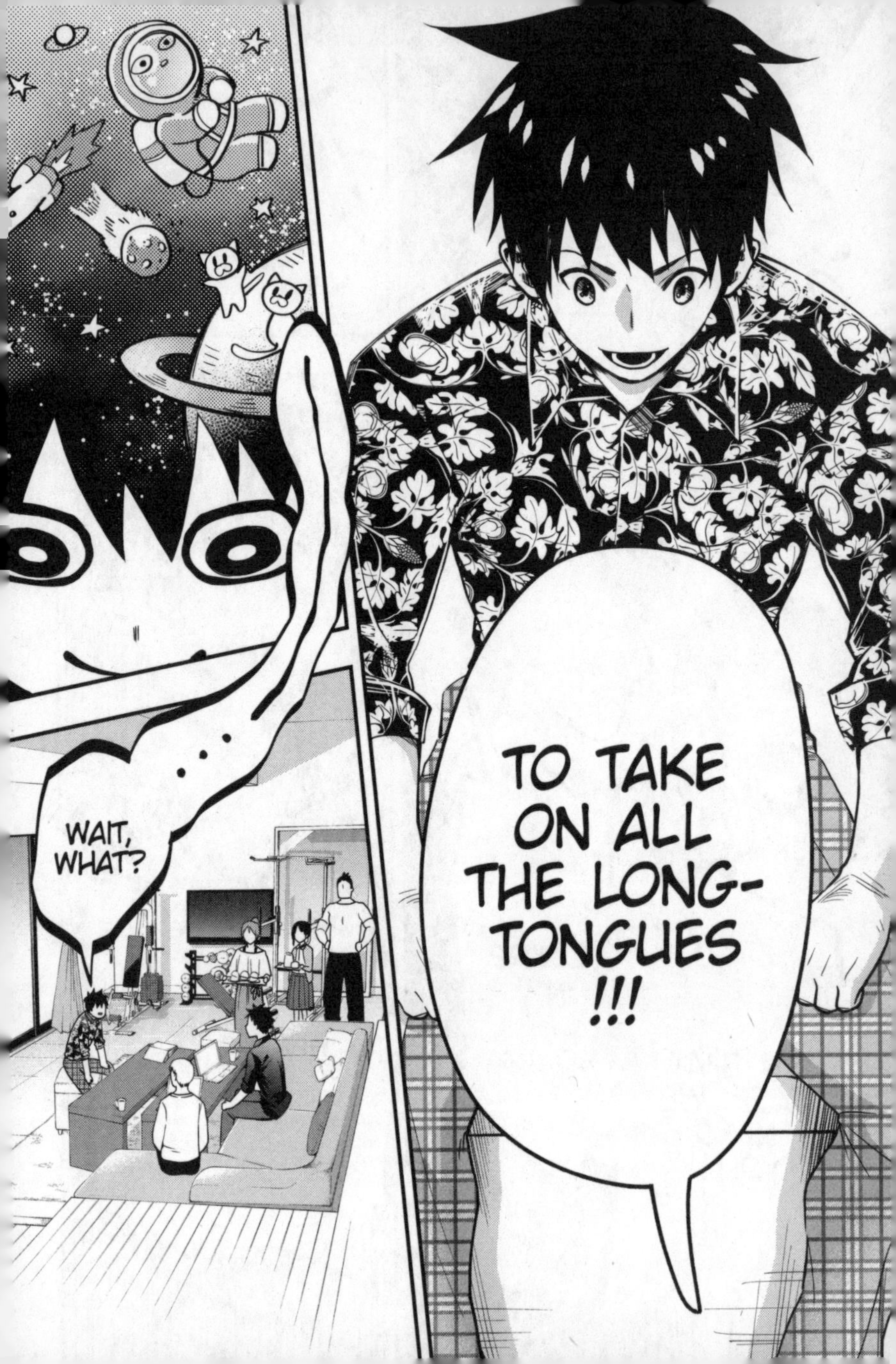
TO TAKE ON ALL THE LONG-TONGUES !!!
...
WAIT, WHAT?

CALL TO ADVENTURE!

DEFEATING DUNGEONS WITH A SKILL BOARD

4

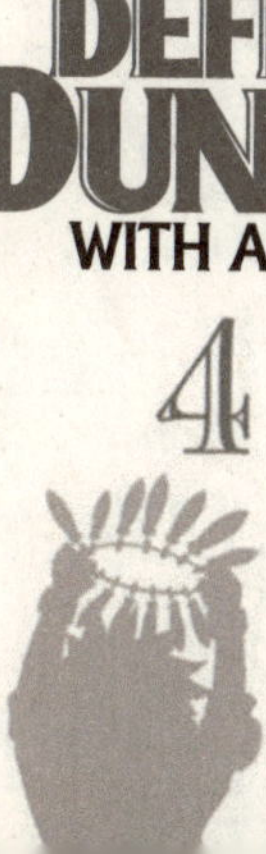

CALL TO ADVENTURE!
DEFEATING DUNGEONS
WITH A SKILL BOARD

4

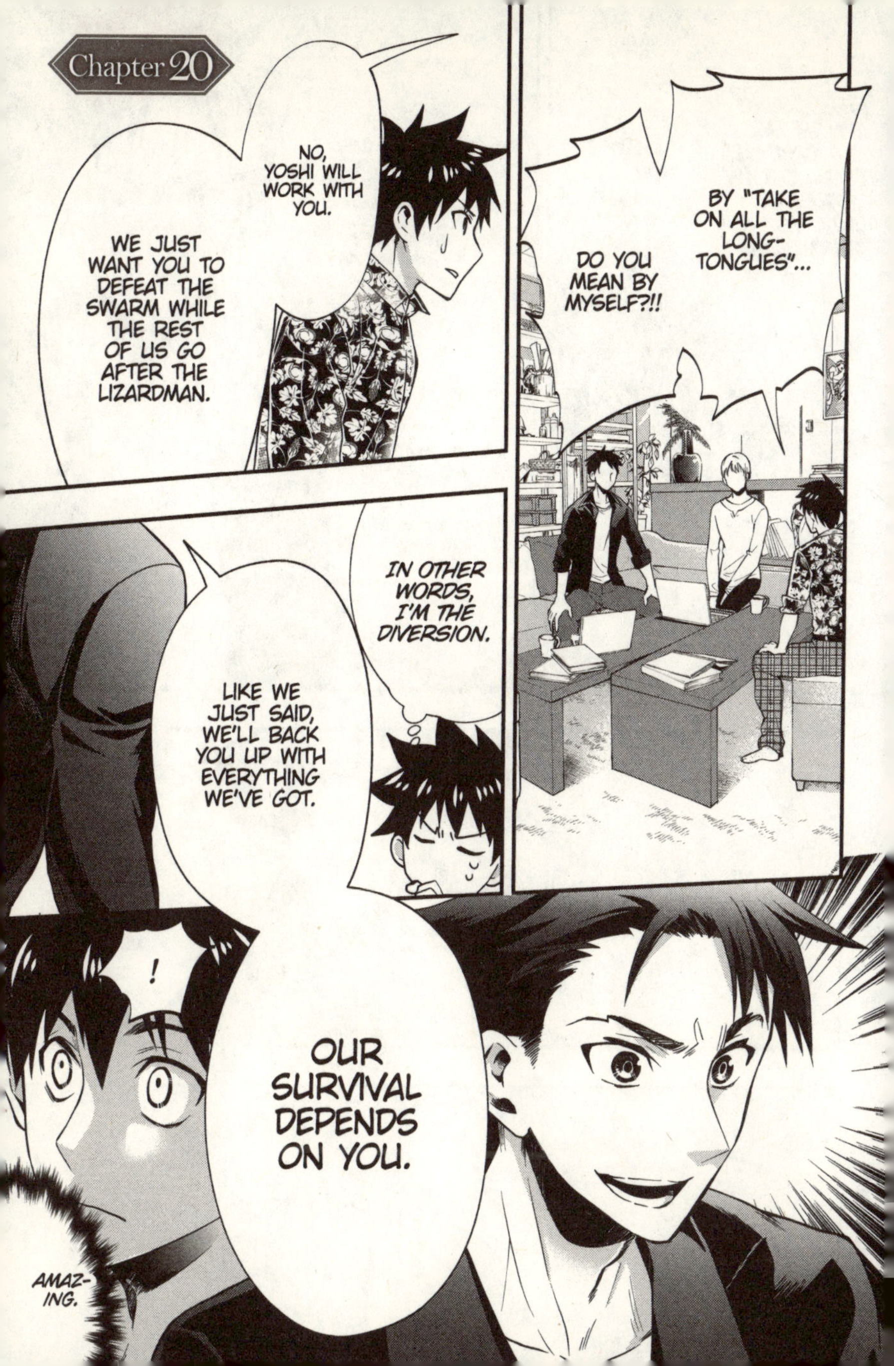
Chapter 20
BY "TAKE ON ALL THE LONG-TONGUES"...
DO YOU MEAN BY MYSELF?!!
NO, YOSHI WILL WORK WITH YOU.
WE JUST WANT YOU TO DEFEAT THE SWARM WHILE THE REST OF US GO AFTER THE LIZARDMAN.
IN OTHER WORDS, I'M THE DIVERSION.
LIKE WE JUST SAID, WE'LL BACK YOU UP WITH EVERYTHING WE'VE GOT.
OUR SURVIVAL DEPENDS ON YOU.
!
AMAZ-ING.

KAGEMITSU ISN'T LOOKING DOWN ON ME FOR BEING INTERMEDIATE. HE'S TREATING ME AS AN EQUAL.

NO WAY I CAN SAY NO!

ESPECIALLY SINCE THIS IS A CHANCE TO GAUGE MY STRENGTH AGAINST A RANKER'S!

HE'S AWARE OF HIS FAME, TOO. THAT'S HOKKAIDO'S TOP RANKER FOR YOU.

I UNDERSTAND.

WE'RE AIMING TO EXTERMINATE THE MONSTER SWARM IN SEVEN DAYS.

UNTIL THEN, WE'RE GOING TO GET YOU USED TO FIGHTING LEVEL 10 MONSTERS.

WE'LL START ON LEVEL 8 TOMORROW.

DON'T LOSE FOCUS JUST BECAUSE IT'S NOT THE REAL FIGHT.

GOT IT!

OKAY!

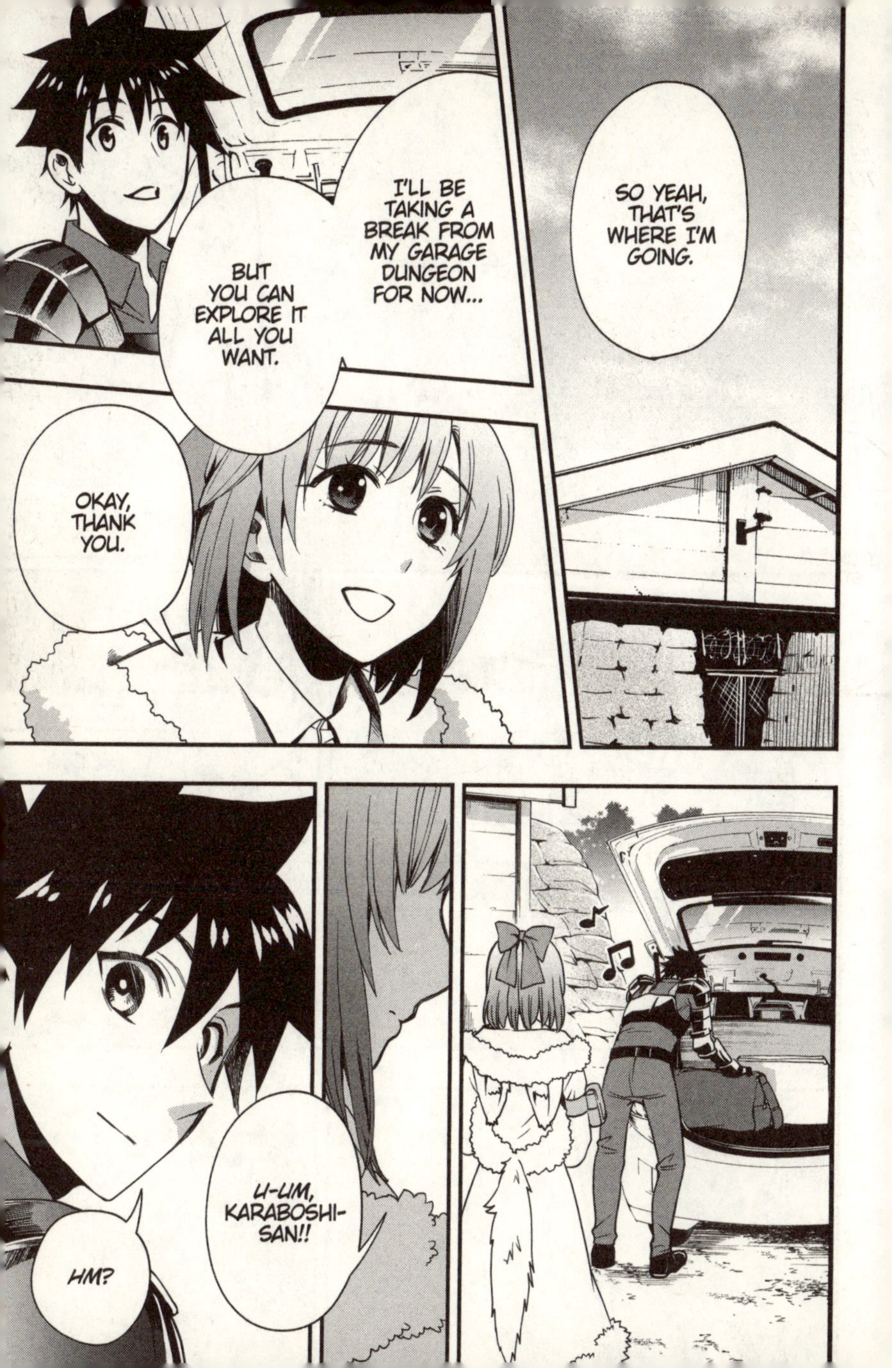
SO YEAH, THAT'S WHERE I'M GOING.
I'LL BE TAKING A BREAK FROM MY GARAGE DUNGEON FOR NOW...
BUT YOU CAN EXPLORE IT ALL YOU WANT.
OKAY, THANK YOU.
U-UM, KARABOSHI-SAN!!
HM?

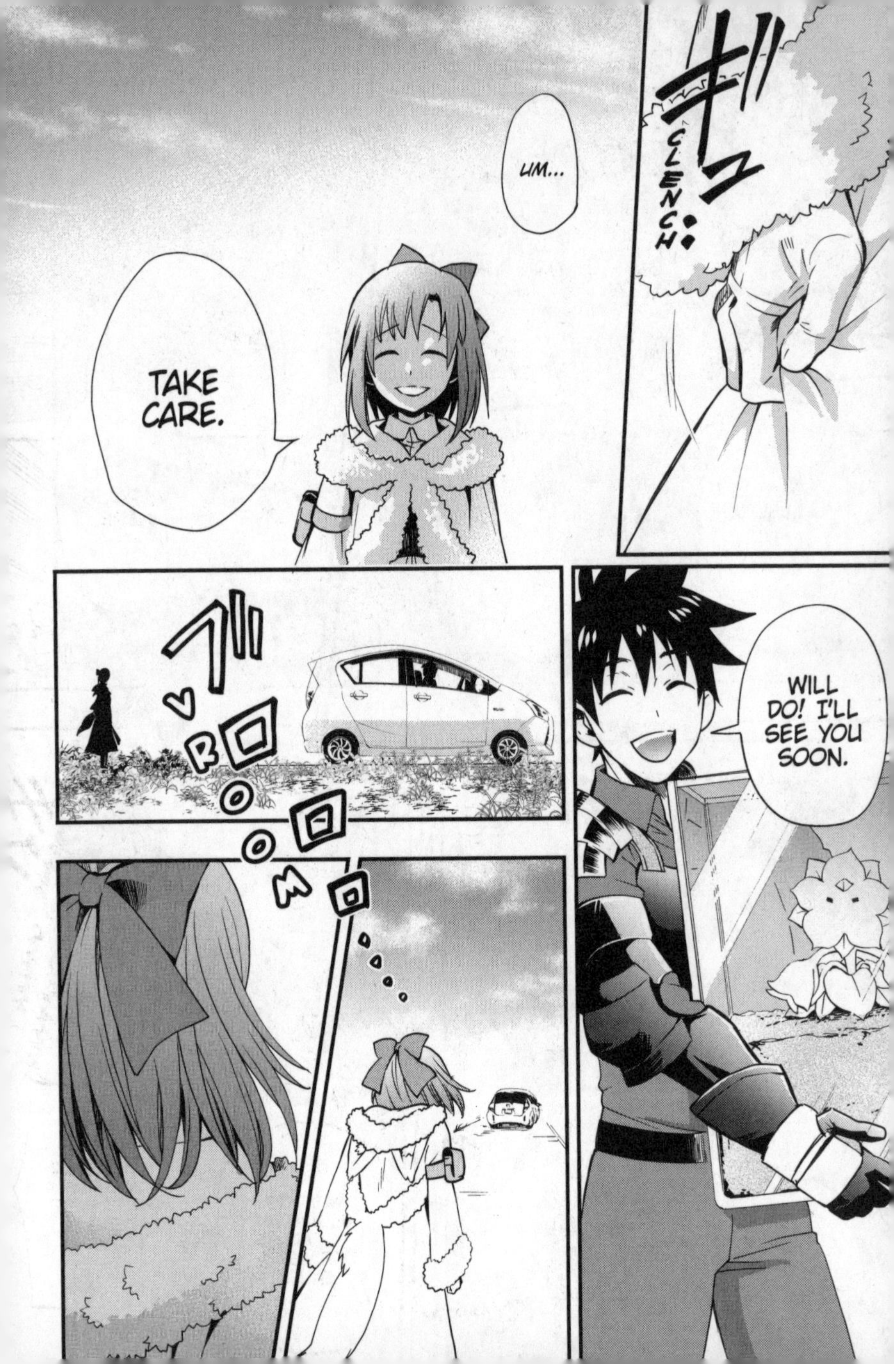
ギュ
CLENCH
UM...
TAKE CARE.
WILL DO! I'LL SEE YOU SOON.
ブロロロ
VROOOM...

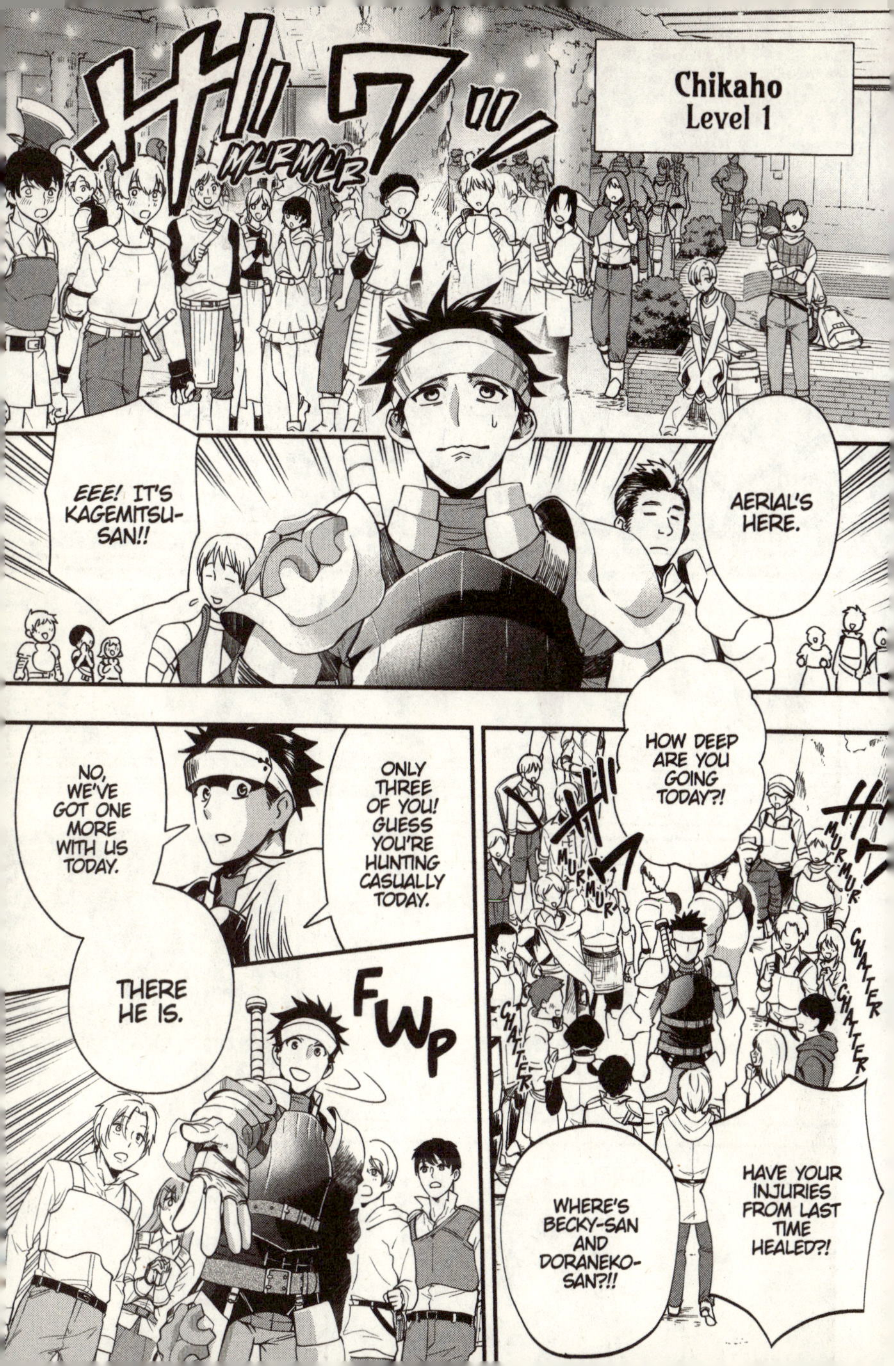
Chikaho Level 1
MURMUR
AERIAL'S HERE.
EEE! IT'S KAGEMITSU-SAN!!
HOW DEEP ARE YOU GOING TODAY?!
MURMUR
MURMUR
CHATTER CHATTER
HAVE YOUR INJURIES FROM LAST TIME HEALED?!
WHERE'S BECKY-SAN AND DORANEKO-SAN?!!
CHATTER
ONLY THREE OF YOU! GUESS YOU'RE HUNTING CASUALLY TODAY.
NO, WE'VE GOT ONE MORE WITH US TODAY.
THERE HE IS.
FWP

HELLO.

GYAAAAH!

I ENVY YOU, DUDE.

I WISH WE COULD SWAP ABILITIES.

HOW? I'M WITH YOU. WHY DON'T THEY SEE ME?

THERE, THERE. DON'T CRY.

STAGGER STAGGER...

YEAH...

KAGEMITSU MAKES HIM STAND OUT EVEN LESS.

OH, RIGHT. THE LEVEL 9 BOSS IS A PET MASTER.
WANNA FIGHT IT TOGETHER?
UM, I'D PREFER TO LEARN THROUGH OBSERVATION.
GOT-CHA.
THE LAST BOSS WENT DOWN SO FAST I DIDN'T EVEN SEE IT HAPPEN.
UH, WHAT?!
YOSHI, VAN, LET'S TAKE THIS THING DOWN!
OKAY.
ROG-ER THAT!
I WON'T MISS IT THIS TIME!
STARE
SUU...
CHAKIIN
ZA
ZA

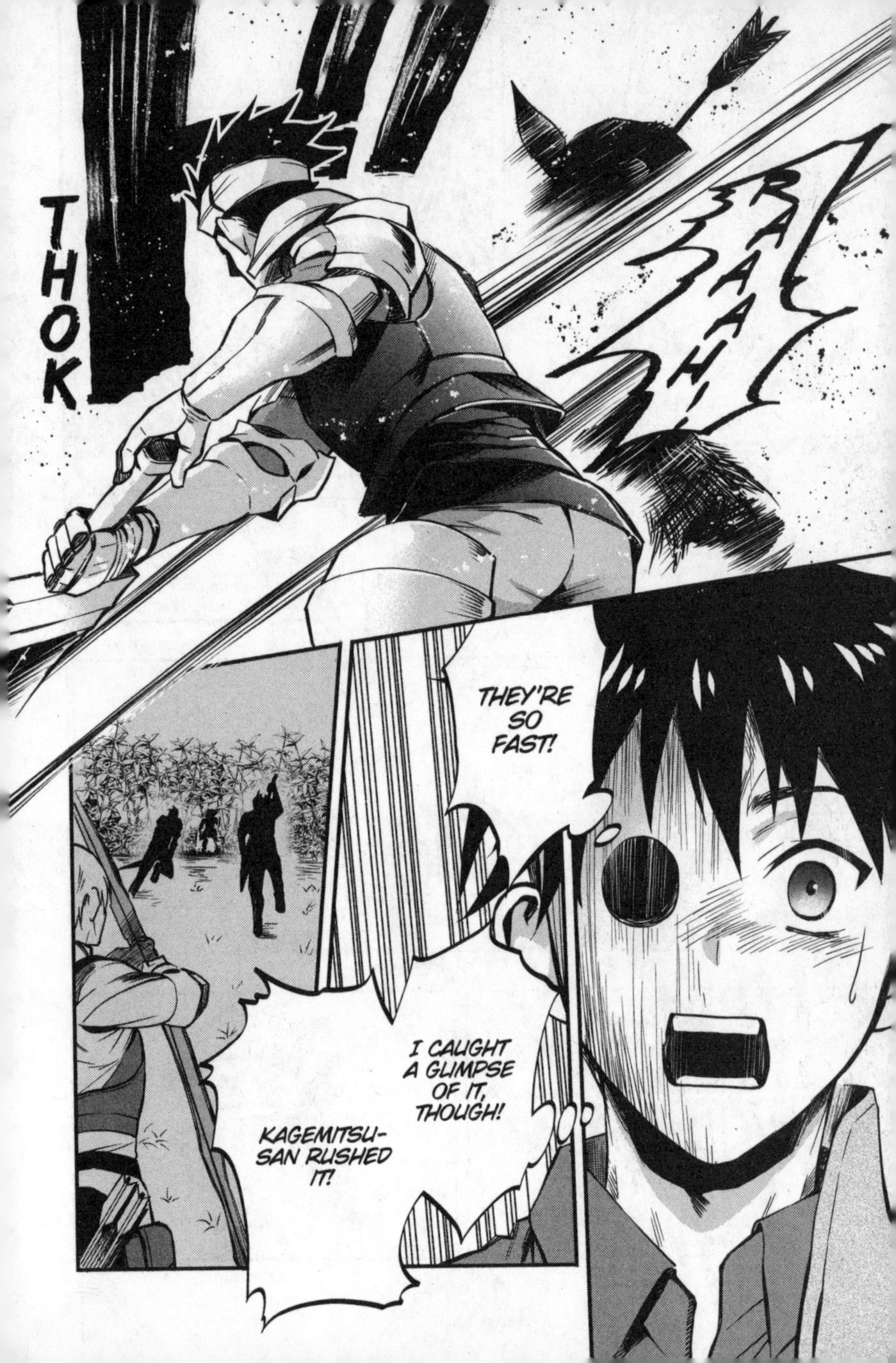
RAAAH!!
THOK
THEY'RE SO FAST!
I CAUGHT A GLIMPSE OF IT, THOUGH!
KAGEMITSU-SAN RUSHED IT!

VAN-SAN SNAPPED THE BOSS'S WEAPON FROM THE SIDE...

BEFORE THE BOSS COULD REGAIN ITS FOOTING! YOSHI-SAN STRUCK IT WITH AN ARROW...

AND KAGEMITSU-SAN DELIVERED THE FINAL BLOW WITH HIS LONGSWORD!

CLAP CLAP

I'VE GOT NOTHING BUT COMPLIMENTS.

HOW'D WE DO?!

CLENCH

I'M ITCHING...

FOR A FIGHT.

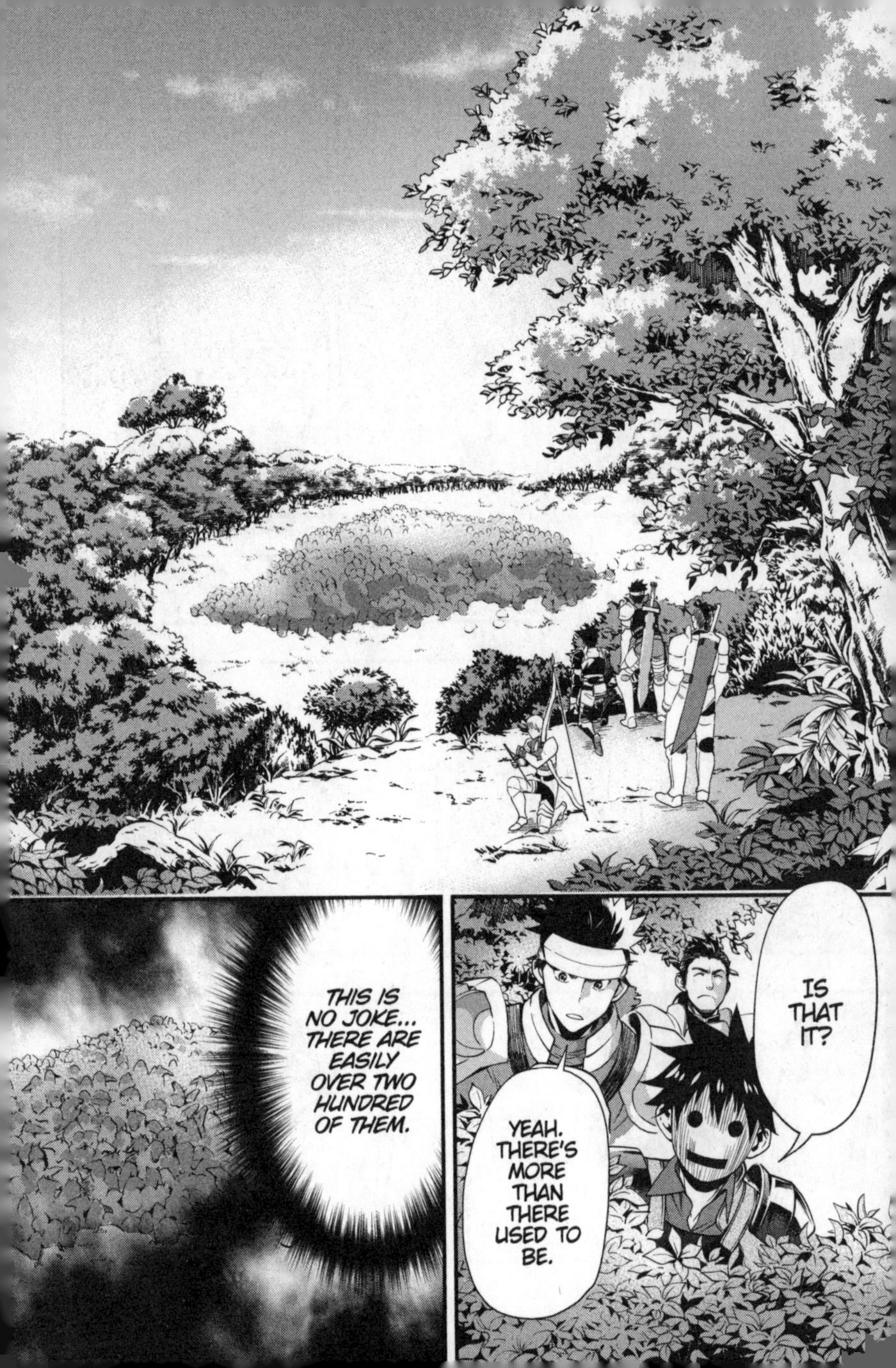
IS THAT IT?
YEAH. THERE'S MORE THAN THERE USED TO BE.
THIS IS NO JOKE... THERE ARE EASILY OVER TWO HUNDRED OF THEM.

I'VE GOT THIS!!

KAGEMITSU-SAN.

WHAT AM I SAYING?

I'M SUPPOSED TO TAKE THOSE ON BY MYSELF?

CAN I REALLY HANDLE THIS?!

HOLD UP. NOT NOW.

YES! LET'S DO IT!

READY TO KICK THIS INTO HIGH GEAR?

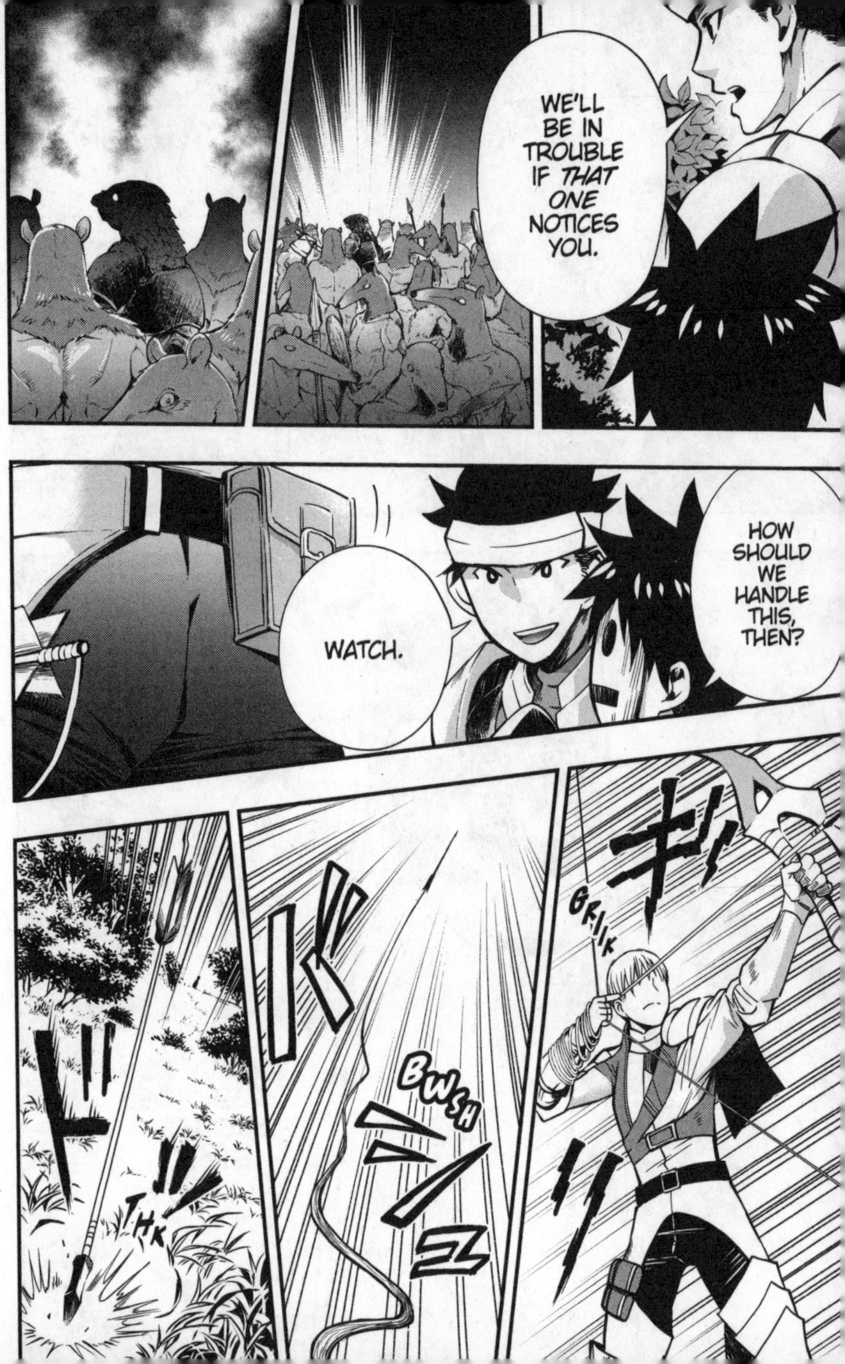
WE'LL BE IN TROUBLE IF *THAT* ONE NOTICES YOU.
HOW SHOULD WE HANDLE THIS, THEN?
WATCH.
GRIIK
BWSH
THK

AH. A FEW OF THEM NOTICED.
SHWP
SHWP
I'LL DRAW THEM AWAY FROM THE GROUP BIT BY BIT.
ONCE THAT HAPPENS, I REEL THE ARROW IN.
AND THAT'S WHERE YOU COME IN.
KILL AS MANY AS YOU WANT.
HE'S SUPER FIRED UP.
DON'T KICK THE BUCKET, YOU HEAR? WOULD REALLY SUCK IF YOU LEAVE US HANGING!
ROGER THAT!
KNCH
KNCH

FIGURES KAGEMITSU-SAN WOULD HAVE THE RIGHT IDEA.
RHEA!
HELP ME OUT HERE!
HERE WE GO!
SHOW ME WHAT YOU'VE GOT!
TIME FOR AN ADVENTURE!

IMPRES-SIVE.
THAT'S NOT HOW I'D EXPECT A SHORT SWORD WIELDER TO FIGHT.
HE'S INTERESTING.
YEAH. I THOUGHT HIT-AND-RUN TACTICS WERE THE FOUNDATION OF SHORT SWORD FIGHTING STYLES...
BUT HE DOESN'T DO THAT AT ALL.
GA-KIIN

HE MAINTAINS SOLID FOOTING WHILE HE DETERMINES WHERE TO BEST STRIKE.
AND HE KEEPS HIS SPINNING TO A MINIMUM.
NOT MANY PEOPLE USE SHORT SWORDS, SO WE DON'T HAVE A LOT OF EXAMPLES...
BUT HE'S CERTAINLY DONE HIS RESEARCH ON THE SUBJECT.
HE'S A NATURAL.
HE'S GOT A GOOD EYE, TOO.
I BET HE COULD REACH LEVEL 12 WITHOUT A HITCH.
YEAH.
STILL...

ABOUT ONE MINUTE PER MONSTER.

YOSHI, HOW LONG DOES HE TAKE?

WHAT DO WE DO? HE'LL DIE AT THIS RATE.

RIGHT.

WE NEED FIVE SECONDS PER MONSTER.

HE TAKES TOO MANY POINTLESS STEPS.

THAT WON'T CUT IT.

WE SHOULD WATCH HIM FOR A LITTLE LONG--

WAS I WRONG ABOUT HIM?

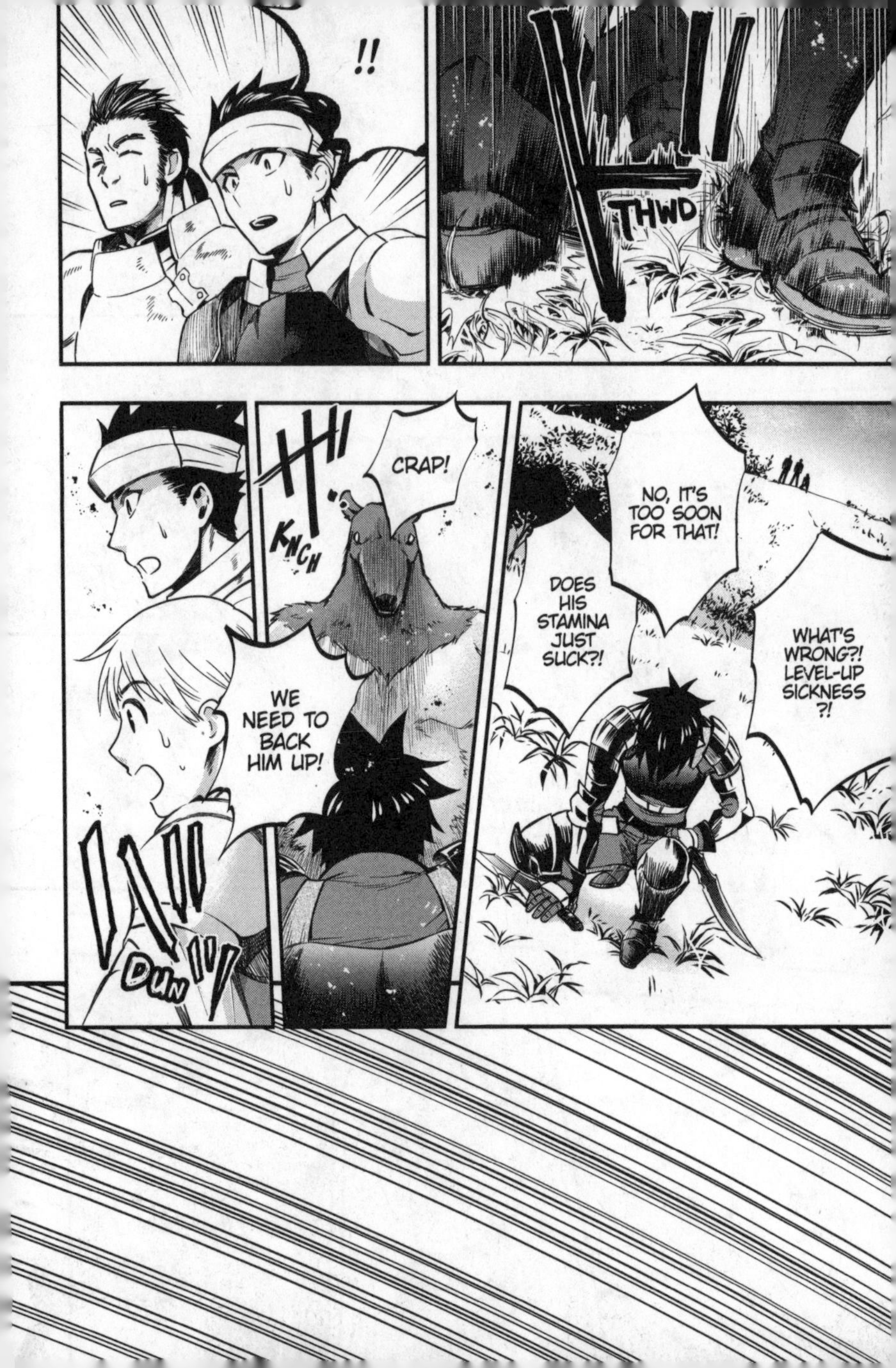
THWD
!!
WHAT'S WRONG?! LEVEL-UP SICKNESS ?!
NO, IT'S TOO SOON FOR THAT!
DOES HIS STAMINA JUST SUCK?!
CRAP!
KNCH
WE NEED TO BACK HIM UP!
DUN

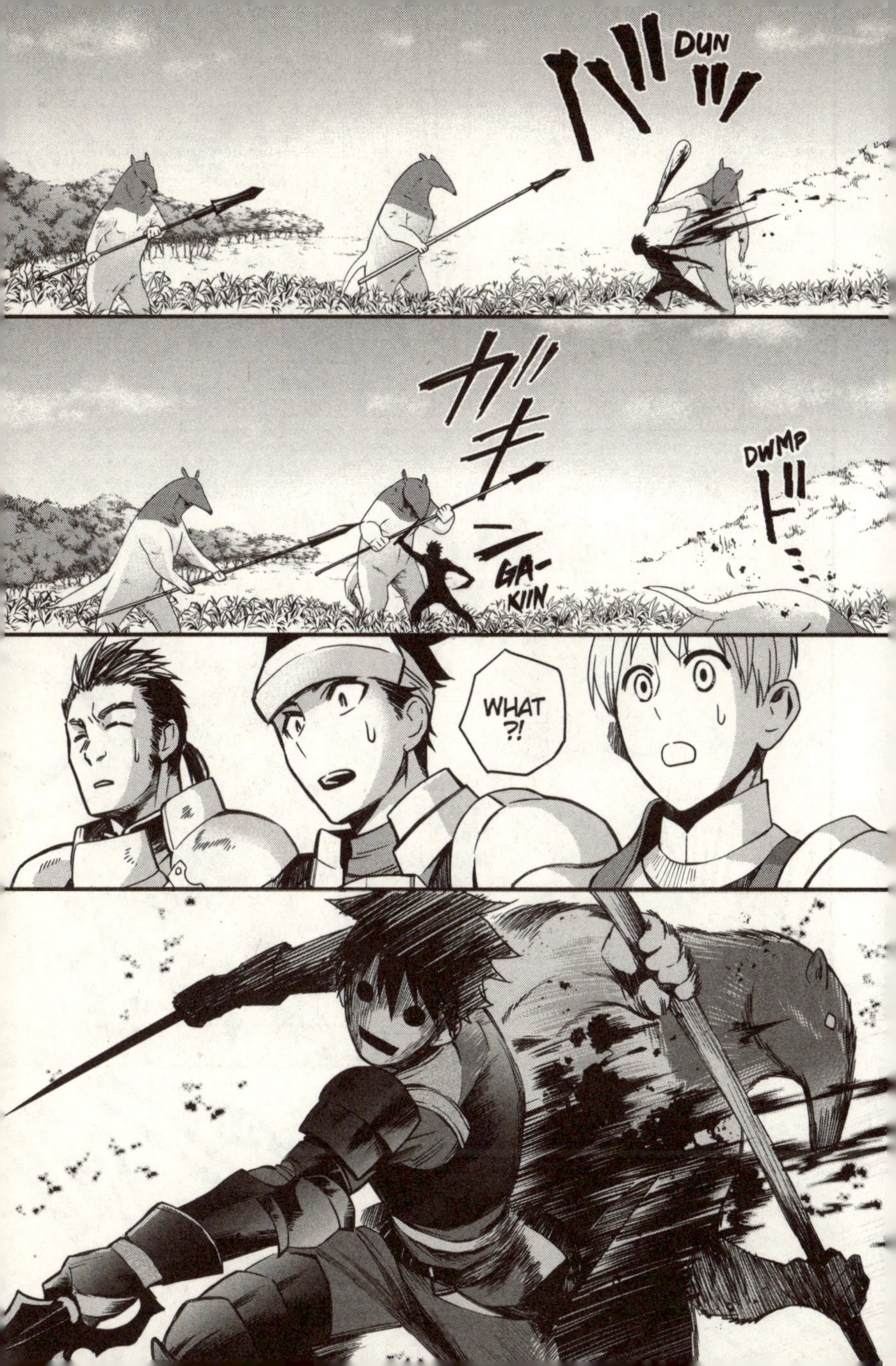
DUN
DWMP
GA-KIIN
WHAT ?!

ZRSH
H-HE DEFEATED THEM.
DWMP
YOSHI-SAN!
HUH ?!
UH, RIGHT!
BRING ON THE NEXT WAVE, PLEASE!
FWP
BWSH

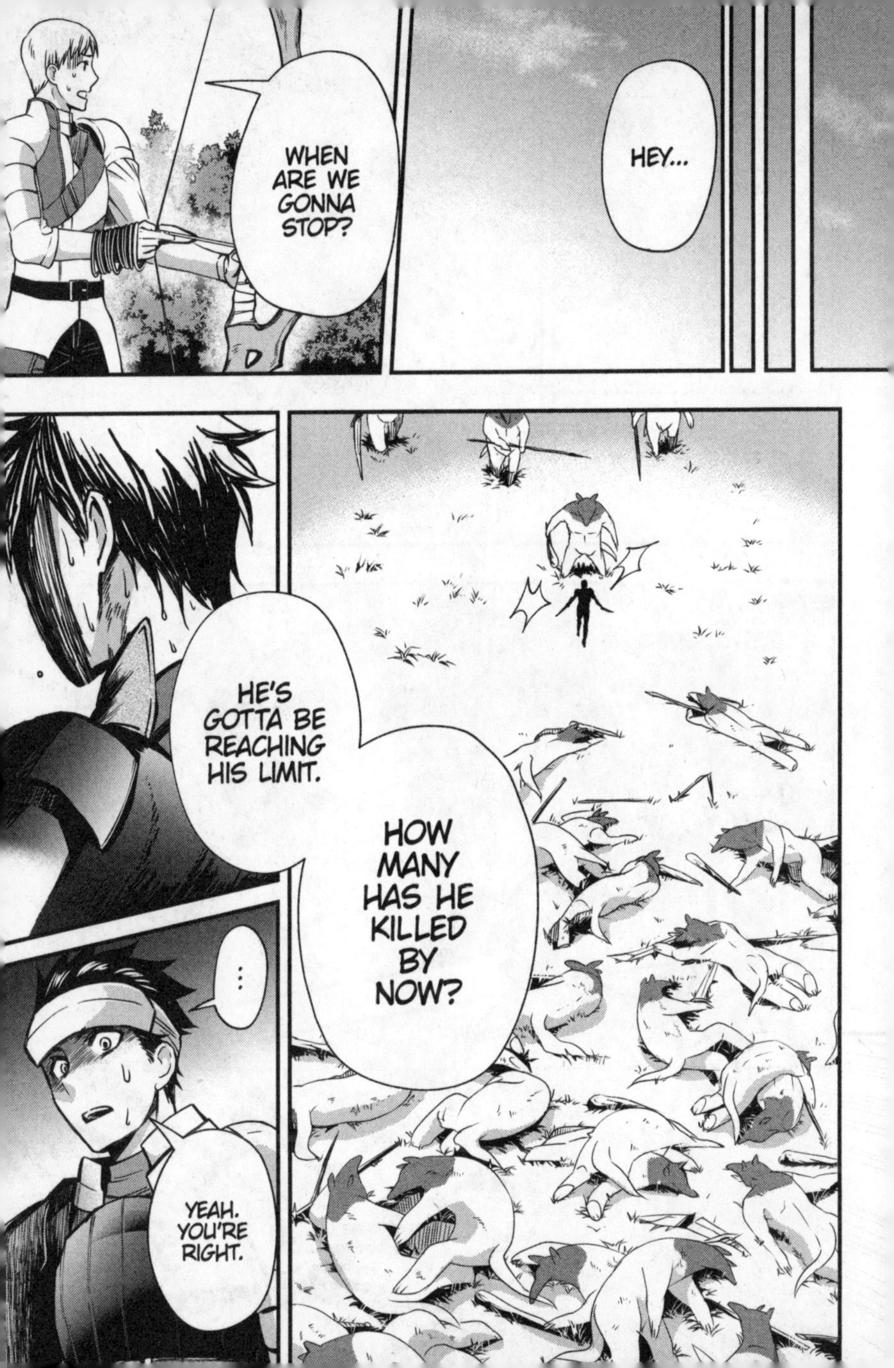
HEY...
WHEN ARE WE GONNA STOP?
HE'S GOTTA BE REACHING HIS LIMIT.
HOW MANY HAS HE KILLED BY NOW?
...
YEAH. YOU'RE RIGHT.

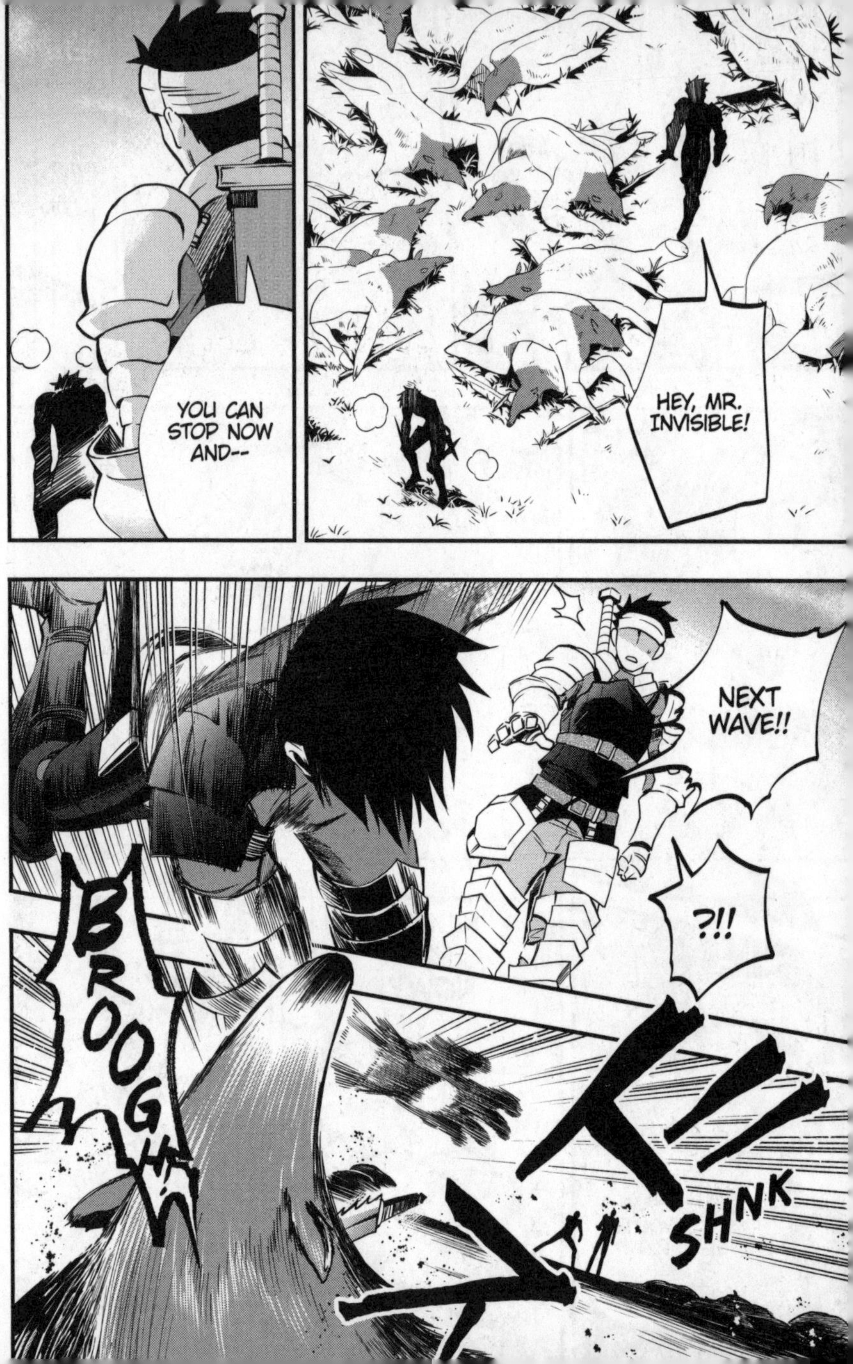
HEY, MR. INVISIBLE!
YOU CAN STOP NOW AND--
NEXT WAVE!!
?!!
BROOGH!
SHNK

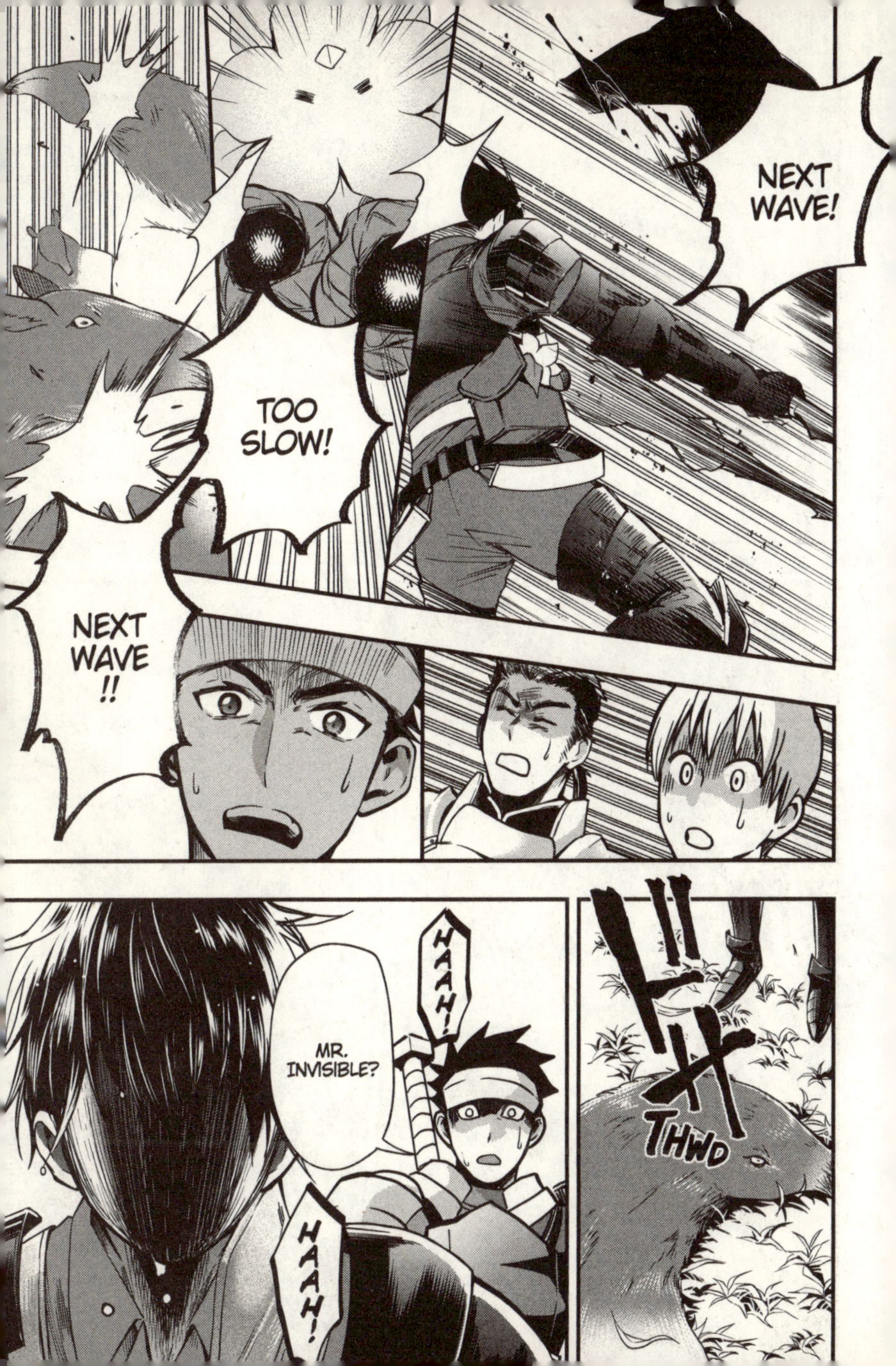
NEXT WAVE!
TOO SLOW!
NEXT WAVE !!
THWD
HAAH!
MR. INVISIBLE?
HAAH!

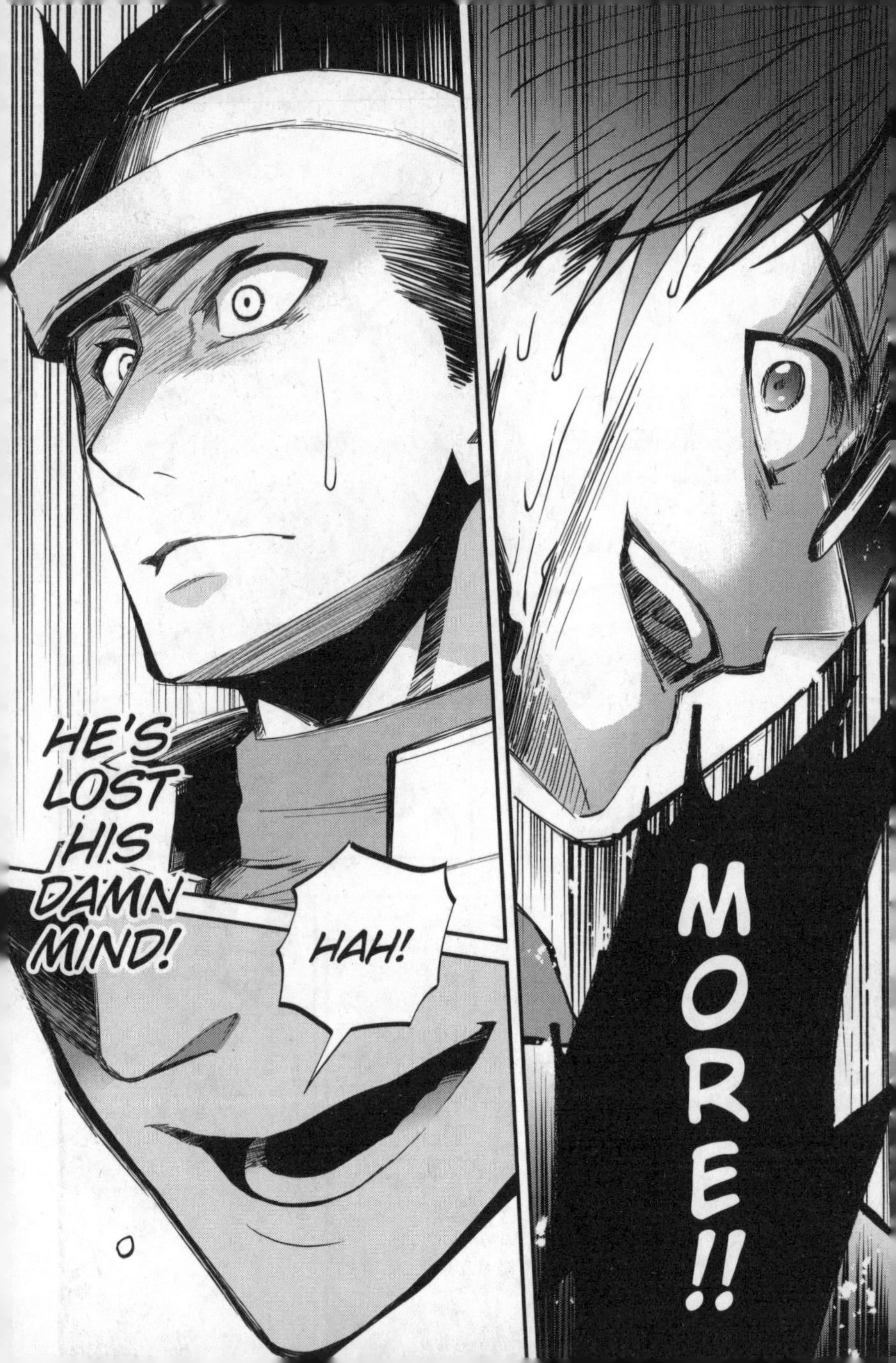
MORE!!
HE'S LOST HIS DAMN MIND!
HAH!

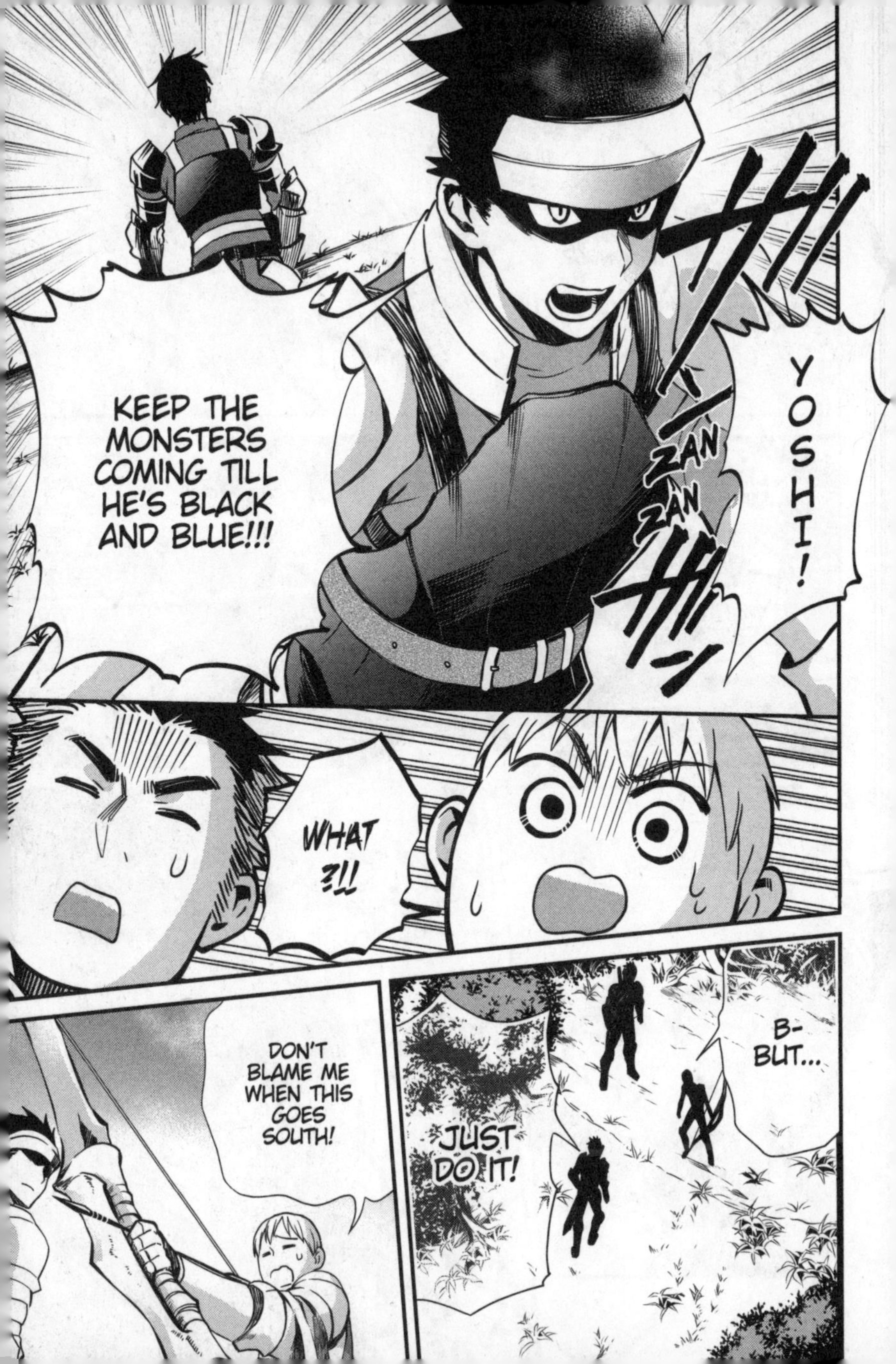
YOSHI!
ZAN ZAN ZAN
KEEP THE MONSTERS COMING TILL HE'S BLACK AND BLUE!!!
WHAT?!!
B-BUT...
JUST DO IT!
DON'T BLAME ME WHEN THIS GOES SOUTH!

ZRSH
HUH?!
TWENTY SECONDS?!
THWNCH
HE GOT FASTER AGAIN!
FIFTEEN SECONDS!
HOW THE HELL IS HE DOING THIS?!
SHIVER
SHIVE
HE'S INSANE.
PROBABLY, BUT...

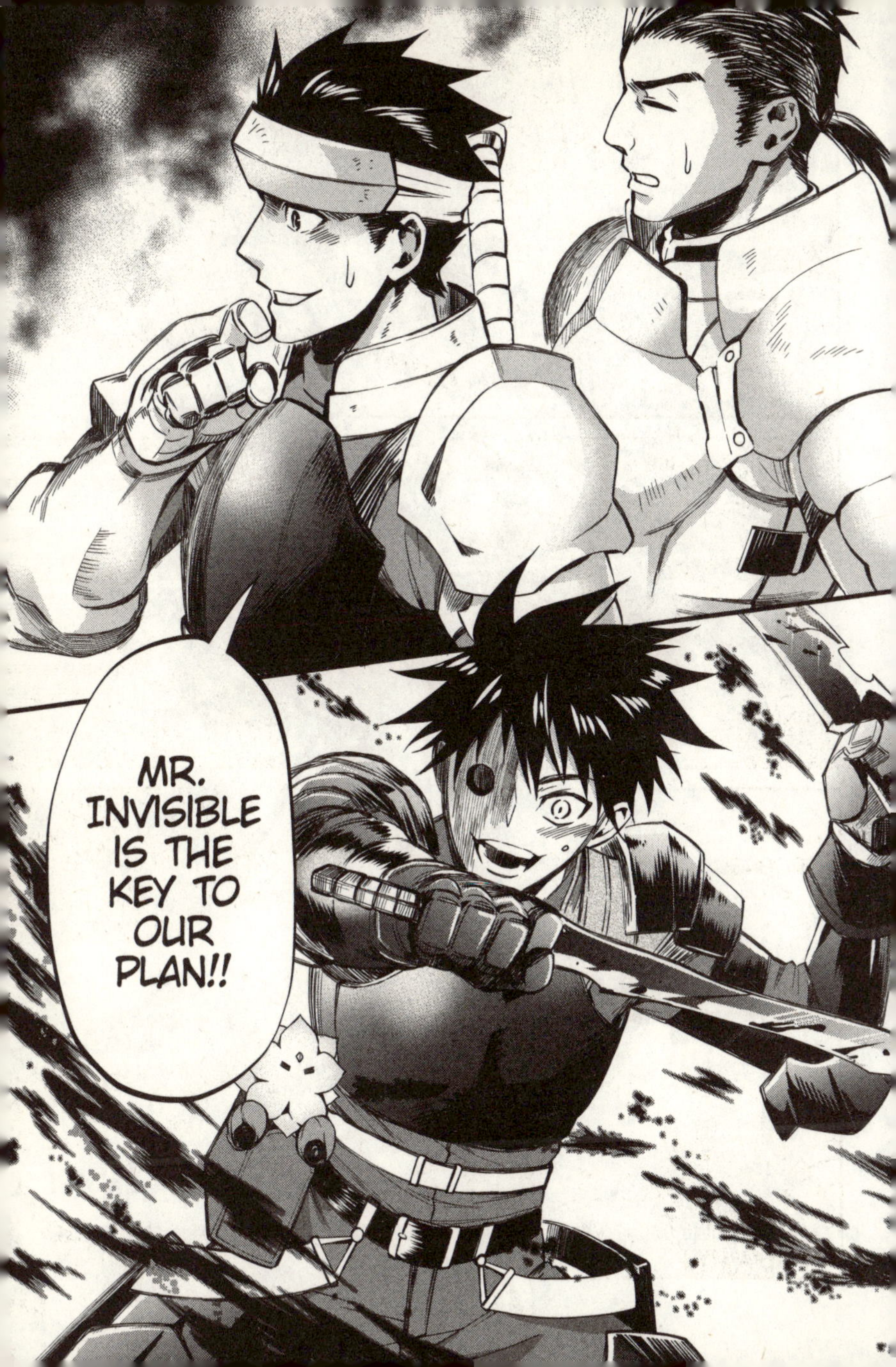
MR. INVISIBLE IS THE KEY TO OUR PLAN!!

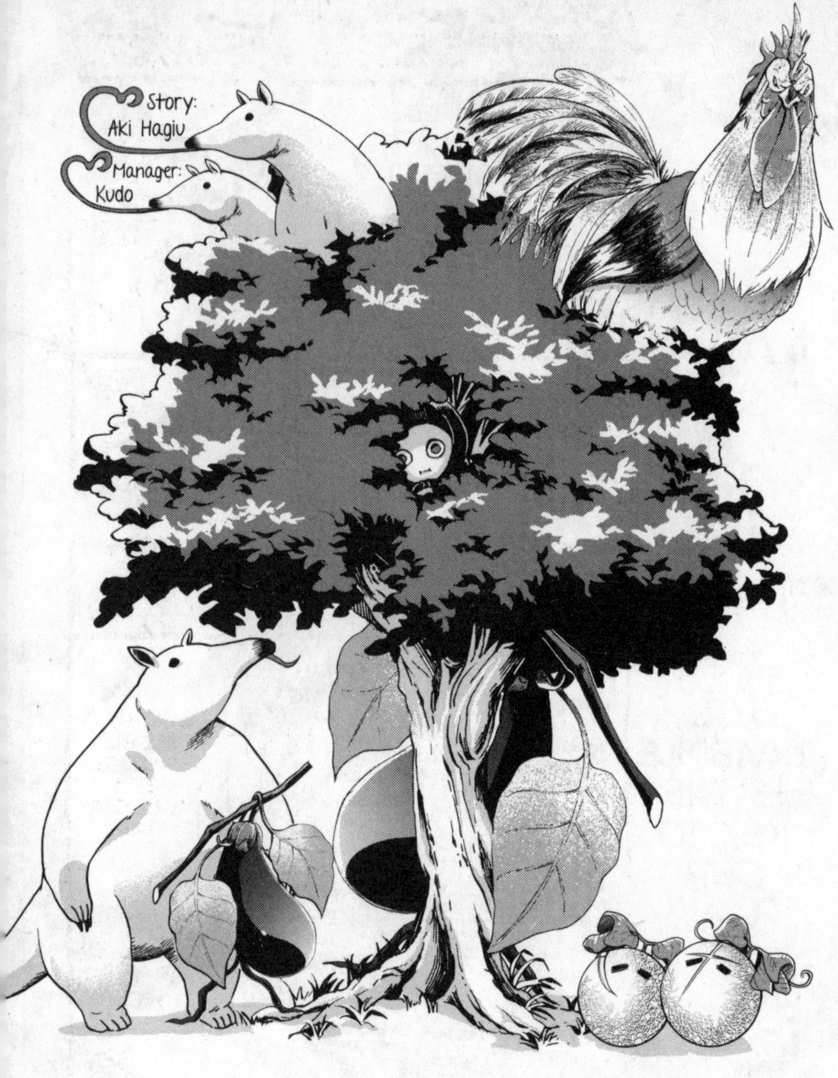
Story:
Aki Hagiu
Manager:
Kudo

SPECIAL THANKS!

JOU-CHAN, HAMA-CHAN, ALL OF MY READERS, AND EVERYONE INVOLVED IN THE MAKING OF THIS BOOK.

SEVEN SEAS ENTERTAINMENT PRESENTS

CALL TO ADVENTURE!
DEFEATING DUNGEONS
WITH A SKILL BOARD
Vol. 4

story by **Aki Hagiu**   art by **RENJI KURIYAMA**   character design by **TEDDY**

TRANSLATION
Morgan Watchorn

ADAPTATION
Maneesh Maganti

LETTERING
Ochie Caraan

COVER DESIGN
H. Qi

LOGO DESIGN
George Panella

PROOFREADER
Kurestin Armada

COPY EDITOR
B. Lillian Martin

SENIOR EDITOR
Jenn Grunigen

PREPRESS TECHNICIAN
Melanie Ujimori

PRINT MANAGER
Rhiannon Rasmussen-Silverstein

PRODUCTION DESIGNER
Christa Miesner

PRODUCTION MANAGER
Lissa Pattillo

EDITOR-IN-CHIEF
Julie Davis

ASSOCIATE PUBLISHER
Adam Arnold

PUBLISHER
Jason DeAngelis

CALL TO ADVENTURE! Defeating Dungeons with a Skill Board Vol. 4
© Renji Kuriyama, Aki Hagiu 2018
All rights reserved.
First published in Japan in 2020 by Futabasha Publishers Ltd., Tokyo.
English version published by Seven Seas Entertainment, LLC.
under license from Futabasha Publishers Ltd.

No portion of this book may be reproduced or transmitted in any form without written permission from the copyright holders. This is a work of fiction. Names, characters, places, and incidents are the products of the author's imagination or are used fictitiously. Any resemblance to actual events, locales, or persons, living or dead, is entirely coincidental. Any information or opinions expressed by the creators of this book belong to those individual creators and do not necessarily reflect the views of Seven Seas Entertainment or its employees.

Seven Seas press and purchase enquiries can be sent to Marketing Manager Lianne Sentar at press@gomanga.com. Information regarding the distribution and purchase of digital editions is available from Digital Manager CK Russell at digital@gomanga.com.

Seven Seas and the Seven Seas logo are trademarks of Seven Seas Entertainment. All rights reserved.

ISBN: 978-1-63858-185-7
Printed in Canada
First Printing: April 2022
10 9 8 7 6 5 4 3 2 1

READING DIRECTIONS

This book reads from *right to left*, Japanese style. If this is your first time reading manga, you start reading from the top right panel on each page and take it from there. If you get lost, just follow the numbered diagram here. It may seem backwards at first, but you'll get the hang of it! Have fun!

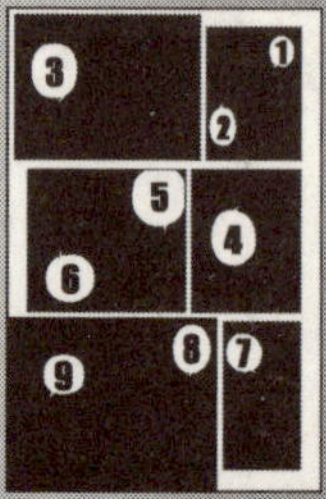

Follow us online: www.SevenSeasEntertainment.com

AKANE & OOISO: HYPOTHETICAL SCENARIO

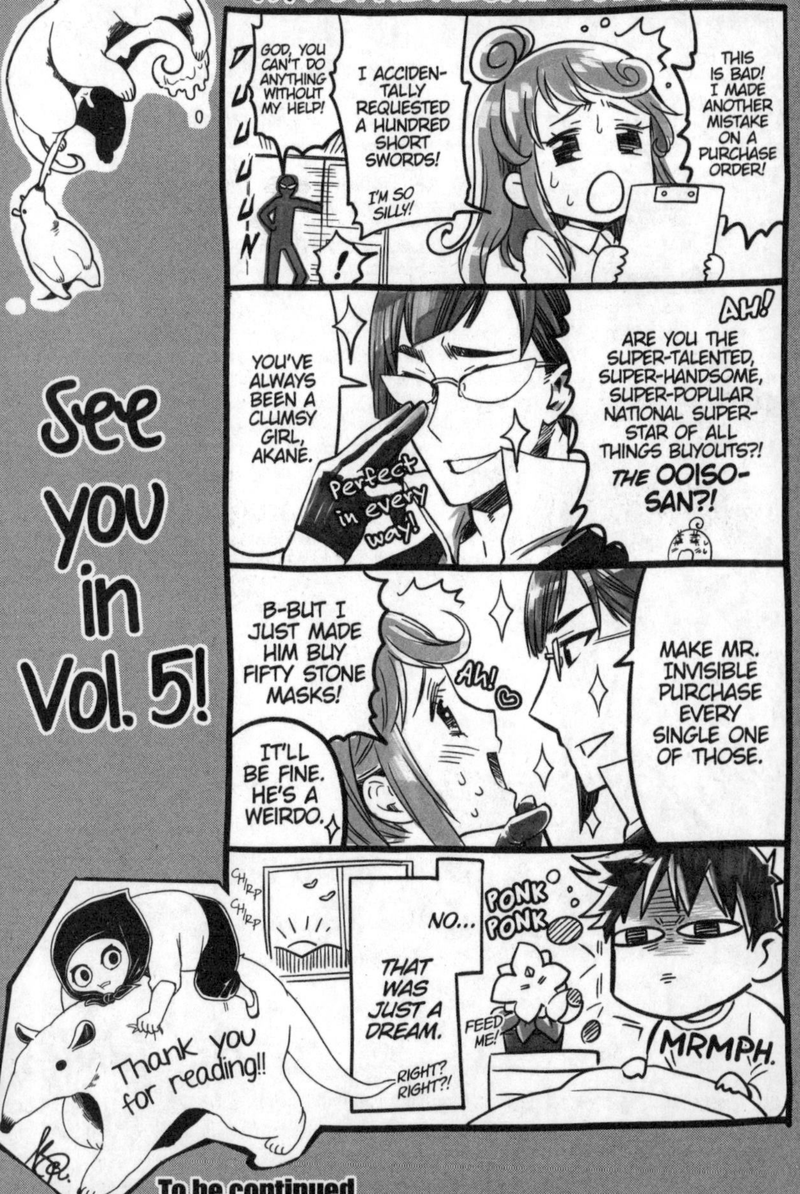
THIS IS BAD! I MADE ANOTHER MISTAKE ON A PURCHASE ORDER!
I ACCIDENTALLY REQUESTED A HUNDRED SHORT SWORDS!
I'M SO SILLY!
GOD, YOU CAN'T DO ANYTHING WITHOUT MY HELP!
DUUUUUN
!
AH!
ARE YOU THE SUPER-TALENTED, SUPER-HANDSOME, SUPER-POPULAR NATIONAL SUPER-STAR OF ALL THINGS BUYOUTS?! THE OOISO-SAN?!
YOU'VE ALWAYS BEEN A CLUMSY GIRL, AKANE.
Perfect in every way!
MAKE MR. INVISIBLE PURCHASE EVERY SINGLE ONE OF THOSE.
B-BUT I JUST MADE HIM BUY FIFTY STONE MASKS!
Ah!
IT'LL BE FINE. HE'S A WEIRDO.
PONK PONK
NO...
THAT WAS JUST A DREAM.
RIGHT? RIGHT?!
FEED ME!
MRMPH.
CHIRP CHIRP
See you in Vol. 5!
Thank you for reading!!

To be continued...